the
opposite
of
music

the
opposite
of
music

janet ruth young

atheneum books for young readers
new york   london   toronto   sydney

Atheneum Books for Young Readers ∗ An imprint of Simon & Schuster Children's Publishing Division ∗ 1230 Avenue of the Americas, New York, New York 10020 ∗ This book is a work of fiction. Any references to historical events, real people, or real locales are used fictitiously. Other names, characters, places, and incidents are products of the author's imagination, and any resemblance to actual events or locales or persons, living or dead, is entirely coincidental. ∗ Copyright © 2007 by Janet Ruth Young ∗ All rights reserved, including the right of reproduction in whole or in part in any form. ∗ The text for this book is set in Sabon. ∗ Manufactured in the United States of America ∗ First Edition ∗ 10 9 8 7 6 5 4 3 2 1 ∗ Library of Congress Cataloging-in-Publication Data ∗ Young, Janet Ruth, 1957– ∗ The opposite of music / Janet Ruth Young.—1st ed. ∗ p.   cm. ∗ Summary: With his family, fifteen-year-old Billy struggles to help his father deal with a debilitating depression. ∗ ISBN-13: 978-1-4169-0040-5 ∗ ISBN-10: 1-4169-0040-3 ∗ [1. Depression, Mental—Fiction. 2. Family problems—Fiction. 3. Fathers—Fiction.] I. Title. ∗ PZ7.Y86528Opp 2007 ∗ [Fic]—dc22 ∗ 2005037122

Definition of "weltschmerz" used by permission. From *Merriam-Webster's Collegiate® Dictionary*, Eleventh Edition © 2005 by Merriam-Webster Inc. (www.Merriam-Webster.com).

"Desiderata" © 1927 by Max Ehrmann, all rights reserved; reprinted by permission of Bell & Son Publishing, LLC.

"Don't Worry, Be Happy" composed/written by Bobby McFerrin and published by ProbNoblem Music.

Excerpts from Robert W. Firestone, "The 'Inner Voice' and Suicide," from *Psychotherapy*, Volume 23, Fall 1986, no. 3, pages 439–447, published by the American Psychological Association. Reprinted with permission.

Article reproduced with permission from "Depression: Electroconvulsive Therapy," April 2005, http://familydoctor.org/058.xml. Copyright © 2005 American Academy of Family Physicians. All Rights Reserved.

"ECT and Brain Damage: Psychiatry's Legacy" © Eugene T. Zimmer 1999. All rights reserved.

"Psychiatry's Electroconvulsive Shock Treatment: A Crime Against Humanity" by Lawrence Stevens, reprinted from the website of the Antipsychiatry Coalition, www.antipsychiatry.org.

To my parents, Mildred and George Young

ACKNOWLEDGMENTS

Thanks to Lois Lowry and the PEN New England Children's Book Discovery Committee for first seeing the potential of this book; to Jen Hirsch, formerly of Brookline Booksmith, and Lorraine Barry of the Reading Public Library, as well as Charline Lake, Janine O'Malley, Sandy Oxley, Lincoln Ross, Jan Voogd, and Diane Young, for their comments at various stages of the manuscript; and to my editors at Atheneum, Caitlyn Dlouhy and Susan Burke, for their superb guidance and warm support.

part one

HANDS ACROSS THE SEA

Resting one hand on the corner mailbox, I balance different ways on my bike. A stream of cars goes by before I see the school bus.

Our town has changed in the last five years. Some of the new kids from other places think they're too upscale for Hawthorne. When I tell Mom this, she thinks I'm misinterpreting the signals. She says I should be attuned to regional differences, that in other parts of the country people have different ways of approaching one another and making new friends. She says I should think of myself as an anthropologist, studying various subcultures of the United States and never forming a value judgment that says my way is better. But I think that if someone sits next to you in class for three weeks and never says anything, the message isn't regional boundaries. The message is they don't want to know you.

Gordy is the big exception. When I wave to the bus driver, Gordy hops down the steps with his jacket over his shoulder, his backpack and music case in the other hand. I don't have much planned. We're going to practice for a vocabulary test, but that won't take long.

"So that's your bike," he says.

"Want to ride it? I could carry your stuff."

"No, thanks."

I like to watch and evaluate the new people who come into town. I've been watching Gordy. In my eyes he is royalty. He is always in his element. He absorbs goings-on without alarm. His hair is always exactly the same length, as if he gets it cut every Tuesday and Thursday. I like to look for people to admire. Otherwise, how will you know who to become?

While Gordy is outstanding in the good sense of the word, I sometimes wonder whether I stand out in the bad sense. My arms and legs seem to grow longer every week, and I am starting to suspect that I may bob up and down excessively when I walk. I say this because a few days ago there was an incident in which I was passing a group of new kids on my way to class and without saying anything they all started bobbing, as if on a prearranged signal. And some of the kids have started calling me Bob.

I wonder what Gordy will think of the house. Our front

door is bright orange, with a brass door knocker in the shape of a salamander. On the door we have an artist's palette dotted with hard, shiny puddles of tint, which my sister Linda made from wood scraps. She also painted our name and house number—Morrison 32—in medieval letters on a white rock at the foot of the driveway. Members of my family try hard to be distinctive.

Dad's Neon is in the driveway. The palette clatters when I open the door.

"Hey, Dad?" I call. "What are you doing home?" Mom is still out. It's two-thirty and she usually doesn't get home from work until four.

But Dad doesn't come to the door as he normally would if I brought someone home. We hear his footsteps at the far end of the house.

"Dad," I say again. Then I see him go by, looking straight ahead, like he needs something from the other end of the house. He's rubbing his hands and whistling between his lower teeth.

"Hi, Mr. Morrison," Gordy says. Dad sees us but doesn't acknowledge us in any way. Gordy and I have stopped within two feet of the door. Something tells me not to go farther. Lately Dad has seemed worried. But he looks even worse than when we left him this morning. I realize, without entirely knowing what it means, that he probably never left for work.

"Dad, I'm home. Gordy's here."

Dad passes by again. The whistling is not like he's enjoying whistling but like he has to whistle. I don't detect a tune.

"I'm sorry, Gord, I guess my father isn't—"

Gordy steps into the living room, into the square of white couches and chairs Mom calls the conversation area. "Mr. Morrison, did you lose something?"

Dad doesn't acknowledge him.

"I can help you look. You know," Gordy continues, "sometimes when you lose something, you keep looking in the same places over and over again, and a stranger can be the best person to help you find it."

"I'll—" I move past Gordy into the hall to see if I can intercept Dad. Dad is known for riddles and charades. It looks like he's pantomiming "chase," "mechanical," or "shooting gallery."

"Dad," I plead, "stop! Talk for a few minutes. Gord, I don't think my father feels like talking. Maybe we should turn around and . . ."

But just as I suggest going, Gordy stops watching Dad and turns to me. Gordy, so superb in ways both like and unlike me, youngest co-captain ever of the All-State Band. Who has performed twice on the White House lawn, and who I hoped to make into a friend.

"Is that Sousa he's whistling?" Gordy asks. "'Hands Across the Sea'?"

I had expected both Dad and Mom, when they got home from work, to greet Gordy the way they greet my friend Mitchell. Dad usually has a joke, a riddle, a quote of the day, or a piece of music that he wants Mitchell to hear. Of course, my parents have known Mitchell for fifteen years, and they don't know Gordy at all, so it wouldn't be the same. And they might sense how exceptional Gordy is (champion French horn player, youngest co-captain ever of the All-State Band, two-time performer on the White House lawn), and that could make them, especially Mom, eager to impress.

But walking away?

At breakfast this morning, whenever Mom spoke to Dad, it took him a few seconds to answer. It seemed his mind was chasing something. And now it seems his body is following his mind. Whatever his mind was chasing was so important that he stayed home from work and chased it all day.

"Sorry, Gord," I say. "I guess my father is a little . . ."

Gordy nods before I even say the word "preoccupied."

"I guess we should just be alone right now."

I hand him his coat and backpack. "See you tomorrow?"

"Sorry if I've upset anyone. I didn't mean to." Paralyzed by politeness, he doesn't want to leave without saying—even shouting—good-bye to Dad.

I close the door behind Gordy. Sandbagged by embarrassment. Could someone have prepared me for this? Like Mom? Sometimes she goes on about a topic until you could strangle yourself. Other times she says nothing when it could be important.

Or does she even know? I sit in the chair nearest the door and wonder what in the world I'm going to say to Dad.

DO NO HARM

A few days later Mom calls Dad's office to negotiate some sick time. Then she schedules a physical exam for Dad.

"I hope this guy knows what he's doing," she says.

Mom has hated doctors ever since what happened to her mother, Grandma Pearl. Grandma thought she had the flu. Her face turned the color of driftwood. Cancer was spreading under the whimsical picture sweaters Grandma always wore.

Mom wanted to bring Grandma Pearl to our house. There Mom could set up a hospital bed in the living room, stroke Grandma's hand, spoon-feed her fruit cocktail, and play easy-listening jazz at low volume. But the doctors kept devising new treatments.

I visited the hospital as often as I could. Zonked on painkillers, she still knew who I was. I read aloud from her collection of back issues of *Ladies' Home Journal*. "Here are the Fourth of July centerpieces, Grandma. Which one do you like the best?" She said that she saw Grandpa Eddie on the ceiling, repairing a carburetor in the nude. "Tell him to put some clothes on, Billy," she said. "He's going to injure himself." The other woman who shared her room coughed so hard I thought she would turn herself inside out like a rubber glove.

A few weeks after the funeral there was a parents' meeting at my school. Sympathetic adults gathered around Mom. Some had also lost their mothers or fathers to cancer. They agreed with Mom about never knowing whether medical treatments were the right decision. Then one woman said to Mom, "Do you know why they put nails in coffins?" When Mom said no, the woman answered, "To keep the oncologists out," and went to get more coffee.

"I'd like to punch that Mrs. Rojas," Mom said in the car on the way home.

Although few people speak about it, the end of life, as I learned in Grandma Pearl's hospital room, is as definite and concrete as the beginning. It is as real an experience as your first day of preschool, for instance. What is the point of living all that time to come to such a wretched end? A science teacher might say that the whole point of Grandma's life was to reproduce, and after that was done, nothing really mattered. But that hospital room remade my grandmother for me against my wishes. For a long time it was impossible to think of her in her own home, doing a mundane, painless thing. Then months later she came back to me, running water over a package of frozen strawberries.

TREATMENT REPORT: DAY 1

Dad's regular doctor said he has to make an appointment with a psychiatrist. Apparently the psychiatrist will perform the necessary repairs on Dad and he will be normal again.

Although Dad has been worrying, pacing, and not eating, nothing showed up in his physical but weight loss and what you would expect from not getting much sleep. So apparently there is some problem with his head. Or mind. Whatever you would call it.

Mom and Dad had an argument about this. "I don't need a headshrinker," Dad said, "I just need some rest!" But the doctor said he has to go.

Mom will take the morning off to drive Dad to the psychiatrist because he's too sleep deprived to get behind the wheel.

CRAZY PEOPLE

We don't know many people who've been to psychiatrists, and when they did it didn't turn out well.

UNCLE JACK

Grandpa Eddie's brother Jack came home nutty from World War II and had to go right into a veterans' hospital, where he stayed until his death, never getting married or having a family. During the war a lot of people visited him, but afterward he was all but forgotten. The only people who continued to visit were Grandpa Eddie and Grandma Pearl, and they said it made them very uncomfortable. "Jack didn't look well," Grandma would reminisce. "God knows what they were doing to that poor boy."

EDIE SARNOFF

My father's brother Marty, before he got married, was dating a woman who went to a psychiatrist. Edie was on medication for extreme mood changes. Sometimes she felt so down that she didn't answer the phone when Marty wanted to check on her, and he would go and bang on her door or throw rocks at the window to get her to let him in. Another time she cleaned out her bank account and dragged Marty on a white-water expedition in the Grand Canyon. There she threw herself off the raft and tried to swim, and Marty and the guide pulled her back in. That night she proposed to Marty at the edge of the canyon. (She had already bought diamond rings for both of them.) The one time she came over for dinner she talked so much no one else could say anything. Marty stopped seeing her when he met Aunt Stephanie. Mom and Dad both felt that Edie was a knockout but more trouble than she was worth.

OTHERS

You hear around school that someone is seeing a psychiatrist or on medication. This often occurs at the time of a mysterious absence. Sometimes people behave differently when they get back. Mostly it's been new kids. They never confide in me.

WHAT'S WRONG WITH DAD?

Two nights after the psychiatrist visit, Mom has finished all her work business, and Dad is trying to nap. I'm at my desk staring at my homework. The house is too quiet. Dad used to blast arias all the time, but now no music is allowed because it irritates Dad's mind. Mom comes to my room.

"Make some space. We need to talk."

I move my bike so Mom and Linda can step inside. Mom sits on my bed. Linda sits in my beanbag chair. I'm in an old office chair, although with the three of us here, it's too crowded for me to spin.

I'd have more space if I moved my bike to the shed, but the shed is leaky and the bike will rust. Instead, I carry the bike morning and night across the off-white carpet in the living room. I can't roll it because it would make tracks. These are the constraints under which I live.

"Don't you look nice, Linda," Mom says.

"Do I?" Linda responds. Linda is almost thirteen. Mom

chastised her once for leaving the house in an outfit that was too tight. Now Linda wears the most voluminous things she can find, just to guilt Mom into taking it back. She would go to school looking like a member of a religious farming sect rather than make things easy for Mom. "It's a matter of principle," she says. She and her friend Jodie find old clothes in the attic crawlspace. Today's look is a ponytail on top of her head and a mechanic's coverall of Grandpa's that says "Eddie" on the pocket. Mom never lets Linda know how annoying this is. They're alike in that way.

Mom is assistant director of our local museum, which is all about the leather industry. There's more to leather history than you would think, she tells people. Often these are people who, she says, are trying to decide her social status. So: Indian techniques for tanning leather. The astonishing range of animal hides used to make leather. The barter value of leather in the colonial period. Mom beats people with this information until they soften up from boredom.

But knowledge is not the whole job. She keeps up the collections and the bookshop. Manages the paid staff and the volunteer docents. Oversees maintenance of "the physical plant." The trickiest part is managing her boss, Pudge. He likes to phone after dinner about museum business while Mom contorts her face into a mask of agony. "Was that the mercurial Pudge?" Dad will usually ask when Mom hangs up the phone. "Was that the irascible Pudge?"

Mom not only works in a museum, she kind of is a museum. She has stick-straight black hair and wears red lipstick. She wears bizarre necklaces, each of which has a story. This one she bought in Mexico when she lived there for a year in college. This one was designed for her by an artist who photographed her wearing it. She stands taller than most men. She is like a museum because she never wants to be forgotten.

"We have a diagnosis," Mom says. "According to the psychiatrist, Dr. Gupta, your father is depressed. Everything he's experiencing—insomnia, anxiety, loss of appetite, tiredness—supports this diagnosis."

Linda wraps her arms around her middle, clutching the extra cloth of Grandpa's overalls.

"I'm not surprised," Mom continues. "Something kept telling me depression, but I refused to accept it. I accept it now. Your father is depressed."

Linda snuffles and pushes her knuckles into her mouth.

"What's wrong, Linda?"

"I know what happens to people who are depressed. They kill themselves!"

"Now where did you get that from?" Mom asks. She reaches down and clasps Linda's ankle.

"We saw a video about it at school. They kill themselves. Sometimes alone, and sometimes in groups, in a suicide pact. One kid even shot himself right in the cafeteria during lunch period!"

"Oh, no," Mom says. "No, Linda, this isn't anything like that. Nothing in that video is going to happen to Dad."

"I saw the movie too," I say. "One teenager intentionally drove into a brick wall with a car full of passengers." The video said not "teenager," but "teen." This was like calling a middle-aged person a "middle." It showed footage from the accident scene—sirens blazing, parents wailing as bodies were removed. I covered my eyes for part of the video, but it was the talk of school that week. The video also discussed copycat suicides, in which a musician or other celebrity kills himself and adolescents duplicate the act, choosing the same date and same method of death, or when one student in a town kills himself and others decide to do the same. While the video played I wondered, *If copycat suicide is such a problem, aren't they worried about giving us ideas?*

But everyone was so excited afterward, talking about this scene or that, that the teachers decided to dismiss us without a question-and-answer period. Among the student body it was universally agreed that the soundtrack was excellent.

"None of that will happen to Dad," Mom says again. Linda climbs on the bed beside Mom, and Mom strokes her hair. "Those kids in the movie, most likely no one cared about them. No one noticed that they were sick. No one tried to help them. In our case, Linda, we have the support we need, and we haven't missed our opportunity. Dad's being treated in plenty of time. And I honestly believe Dr. Gupta knows what she's doing.

"Dr. Gupta says that this kind of illness can come from a change in brain chemistry or from a loss or from a change in living situation that the patient has trouble adjusting to. It's like they're going through a crisis. So Dad will be taking medicine to help his brain, and he's also going to get talk therapy to find out what's going on."

"I have one question."

"What is that, Billy?"

"When will he be better?"

"The medicine should start working in about two weeks."

Linda has curled up under Mom's hand, until she's practically in the fetal position.

"What I need from you right now is input about any problems or difficulties that could be causing stress in Dad's life. Any possibility, Dr. Gupta says, even if it appears unrelated. Let your minds run free. Brainstorm. Think outside the box. Don't censor yourselves."

I turn to a fresh page in my history notebook.

Linda snuffles again. "You're not gonna like what I have to say, Mom."

"That's okay, honey, just go ahead. This is the time to speak freely."

"Maybe he feels *trapped*," Linda says. "Maybe he *never really wanted* a wife and kids. Maybe he'd rather have a totally different life—like be an actor or a race car driver or something."

It's typical that, right after a weepy outburst, Linda is becoming critical again. But Mom's accustomed to Linda's moods. Mom slides the wooden beads along the cord of her necklace, and they make a sound like bones clacking. "Let me reassure you of something, Linda: Your father loves this family more than anything on earth. You should have seen him the day you were born. He said, 'A boy and a girl. Now I have everything I could ever have wanted from life.'"

I look sideways at Mom. "I thought you said not to censor ourselves."

"Well, censor a *tad*. Use your judgment. Linda, I know you wouldn't say something like that unless you were worried and upset. But maybe we can pursue the possibility that he's dissatisfied with *some area* of his life."

I write "dissatisfied," followed by a question mark.

"You know," I point out, "maybe Linda's onto something. What about the fact that Dad never finished art school? Perhaps he thinks of himself as a failure. It isn't anything like those people in the video, but just, you know, a little unhappy, like something is missing. Like things could be better."

"Dad really isn't what you would call successful," Linda agrees. "I mean, compared to some of the other dads, like Jodie's dad. Not that I'm criticizing him or anything."

"Well, he chose his own path," I offer. I heard this once and liked the sound of it.

"That raises some interesting questions," Mom says. "What is success? Perhaps Jodie's dad did build a second garage for his collection of Italian sports cars, and he takes his family on expensive vacations every year, but does he feel successful inside? Is he truly happy with his life?"

"*I* think so," Linda says.

"Well, you just don't know, do you? You can only discover the truth by probing beneath the surface."

In fact, Dad *is* kind of unsuccessful compared to other adults. But he didn't seem to want to climb the ladder of success. He got a job as a draftsman in a company that manufactures store fixtures. He opposed overtime as a matter of principle, tore off his necktie when he stepped into the house, and preferred to spend his extra hours playing tennis, drawing cartoons, and listening to opera.

"Mom, are we poor?" Linda asks.

"No, Linda, not poor, just lower middle class. But we're well educated. I have a master's degree and your father attended one of the most prestigious art schools in the country. That's more important than money."

I suggest a different angle. "Mom, the important point is: Does Dad *think of himself* as successful?"

"He is definitely more successful than Uncle Marty," Linda points out. Marty keeps starting businesses with people, but it seems like either the businesses flop or he gets cheated.

"But possibly less successful than other people he knew in college," I add.

"Well, what do you think they're all doing now?" Mom asks. "I met some of them about ten years back. They were in their late thirties and living in divey apartments with six roommates, eating Beefaroni out of the can. They couldn't even scrape up the money to visit the Museum of Modern Art, although any philistine with twenty bucks in his pocket can see the greatest collection of artwork in the United States or possibly the world. Paradoxical, isn't it? Anyway, success, as I've said, is a highly subjective judgment. How do you define it? Some people believe success just amounts to whether you're happy."

"But Dad isn't happy," I remind her. "That's the problem he's having right now, isn't it?"

I write the word "success." Then I get another idea: *the past.*

"What about Dad's parents? How do they fit into the picture?"

Mom cocks her head. "His parents?"

"What I mean is how he felt when they died. When we couldn't get there in time. Could that be considered a crisis?" Both of Dad's parents, who lived in New York, died when I was eleven. My grandfather went first, suddenly, of a heart attack in the hardware store parking lot while moving lumber into his van. Then my grandmother had a stroke, and we visited occasionally to help care for her. But she took a turn for the worse and the hospital called. Dad left work, and we jumped into the car and raced toward Long Island. The engine overheated on I-95. When we arrived at the hospital she was gone. Linda and I bawled for hours. Dad never shed a tear, but he traded in that car the day after the funeral.

Soon after that, for my twelfth birthday my father got me a three-speed from a used-bike shop. The bike was about fifty years old, painted black, with a two-tone treatment, black and white, on the seat and the back fender.

Dad threw himself into fixing up the bike. We replaced the cracked tires and the gummy chain, hammered bumps out of the rims, and dripped oil into the hub. We rubbed the rust spots from the chrome with steel wool, then waxed the chrome to prevent it from rusting again.

"What will you name your bike?" Dad had asked. "I named my favorite bike Pavarotti. You could call this one Seabiscuit or Rosinante." We were brightening the cloudy paint with buffing compound and a coat of car wax.

"I think I'll just call it Triumph."

"That's a good call."

The brand name "Triumph" appeared five places on my bike: on the tube below the seat in colored squares like a kid's alphabet blocks, in gold letters on the chain cover, in small white letters on the lower tube, and on two coats of arms on the front stem and back fender. With encouragement from all over my bicycle, how could I not triumph?

Now Mom's eyes water. "I don't know, maybe I'm depressed. I haven't felt like myself, anyway, since . . ." She's remembering not only Dad's parents but her own. "The world is a poorer place for the loss of all of them. That whole World War II generation. So brave. You know what they're called now? The Greatest Generation. 'Never give in, never, never, never, never—in nothing, great or small, large or petty—never give in except to convictions of honour and good sense. Never yield to force; never yield to the apparently overwhelming might of the enemy.' Winston Churchill."

"God, now I'm getting depressed too," Linda says, starting to cry again. "How are we going to help Dad if we can't even keep it together ourselves?"

Tears circle the room, contagious as yawning or nausea,

but I'm determined not to give in. I write down the word "family." "Mom, is this kind of thing hereditary? I mean, was there anyone else in Dad's family who had . . . you know, mental problems, that you know of?"

"I'm not sure. Dr. Gupta asked us that too. Maybe I should talk to Marty about it."

Linda lies on her back, staring at the ceiling. "Hey, isn't Dad's cousin Amy a bit, if you'll pardon the expression, nuts?"

"'Nuts' is not a word that we use in this house."

"We used to."

"Well, we don't anymore."

"Okay, I'll try again. Isn't Cousin Amy a bit flaky or a bit off-kilter? The cats, the newspapers, the empty jars and jar lids, the smell? How many cats were there, anyway?"

"I think the population reached as many as thirty-five or more at the point that they were taken away. Now she seems happy with just the seven."

"Ew," Linda says.

"It is a big house," Mom reminds her.

"Let me write that down. And I think I remember Uncle Marty saying that someone else on Amy's side was a klepto-maniac and spent time in prison."

"One of your father's cousins, you mean?" Mom stares. She may never have heard this story. Marty says he finds me easy to confide in. "Could that have been the one who returned a positive RSVP to our wedding but didn't show up? I always thought he was terribly rude. Well, he missed a good meal."

Mom gets up and cracks the door, motioning for silence. "Your father's up. Resume your normal activities. To be continued."

SHADOW

You can see the highway through the slats in the fence behind our house. A tunnel runs under it, where the workmen used to cross back and forth while the road was being constructed. I was forbidden to go inside, but who could resist? A concrete-lined cylinder, cracked in places, rumored to have rats. By the time I had the courage to run through it, I was too tall to get through without stooping, making it a fast, uncomfortable trip with the sound of traffic close to my head. Every kid from the old regime has been through that tunnel and back once. The new ones probably will never even know it's there.

This is the oldest part of Route 128, north of Boston from Hawthorne to Gloucester, where the highway has only two lanes in either direction. The houses on my street were built all on one floor, and they're all identical, although some are turned this way or that on the winding, hilly road. When I was little, you could walk into any house blindfolded and be able to find a box of cornflakes, a piece of chalk, or a Nerf ball.

From the driveway (no garage, no carport, two economy cars), you walk in the front door (no hallway, foyer, or vestibule) directly into the living room. Here is a big plate-glass window ideal for leaning on for hours, when you were small, in case a rabbit or anything went by, and leaving your hand and lip prints on the glass like white stage makeup.

A dining room with crank-out windows is behind the living room, and if it's summer you have to decide whether to be cool and hear the highway noise or enjoy a sweaty silence. Next to that is a kitchen that looks into the living room over a partial brick wall topped by metal bars, so your mother could see what you were doing if it got too quiet. At one end of the house are a woody den with built-in spaces for books and your family's one TV, then a small cement-floored room for your tools, sports equipment, winter boots, cleaning supplies, and so on. This room contains your oil tank, your clothes dryer and ironing board, and a pull-down ladder for reaching the attic crawlspace to get toys you've outgrown but like to visit, Halloween costumes, and all your grandparents' things. Also a pink kitchen table with black legs, where your father keeps an ancient suitcase full of small hardware parts that he never bothers to sort. And which you open sometimes, on your own, to crunch the parts with both hands and hear them clank—like a sea that someone drained the water from, leaving only shells.

At the other end of the house are two junior-size bedrooms and a hall bathroom, and one big bedroom with its own sink and toilet. Outside are a bicycle shed, a garden shed, and a patio made of concrete blocks.

All perfectly adequate, you would think. But then in September, our uphill neighbors built an addition, a second-story bedroom the length of the whole house and a mammoth garage with a separate apartment above it for their son who is not much older than me, and just as the builders were finishing the parents' balcony and the appliance store truck was pulling up with the son's gas grill, our house was eclipsed. Mom stood in the shadow beside her rosebushes, shaking a fist at the neighbors' house (although she knew they weren't home at the time).

"How could they do this to us?" she wailed.

I'm not sure, but I think this shadow could be contributing to our problems.

WORLDPAIN

welt·schmerz \'velt · shmərts\ *n, often cap* [G. fr. *Welt* world
+ *Schmerz* pain, fr. OHG *smerzo*; akin to OHG *smerzan*
to pain—more at SMART] (1875) 1: mental depression
or apathy caused by comparison of the actual state of
the world with an ideal state

Intellectual, no? It would be just like Dad to go for that
one.

NOCTURNE

Just after one a.m. sounds begin in the hall. Two voices so familiar they could originate in my own chest. The rubbing swing of the door over carpet, and the swoosh of two sets of slippered feet. My curtains are partly open, and street-lights are reflected in our first snow. A column of light falls over my bed, illuminating me, Triumph's front fender, and a thumbtacked Escher print of flying fish in formation, like torpedoes.

The people switch lights on as they move through the house. These new lights seep under my door. The other lights cause my window to darken and my column of light to fade.

In the kitchen, the woman talks more than the man. She speaks mostly in whispers. The man isn't a good whisperer. When he thinks he's whispering, he's just talking but adding breath sounds to it.

The refrigerator door opens and closes. A pan rattles

on the stove. Liquid is poured. The fridge door opens and closes again. The burner clicks several times as it heats up. One person stirs the pot while the other pads across the kitchen floor. A cabinet door opens. Dishes click. Liquid is poured from the pot. The kitchen light goes out. Other lights go out. My window gets brighter. My column gets bigger. They stop just outside my door.

"Billy's asleep," Mom whispers.

"Good," says Dad. "Billy's asleep."

MACARONI

I'm resting my head over a plate of macaroni and cheese when someone knocks my elbow.

"Hey!"

Mitchell Zane and Andy Bock sit down with their trays. Mitchell slides the wrapper to one end of his straw, where it crumples into a miniature Japanese lantern.

"You fell asleep in chemistry," he says.

"Did anyone notice?"

"Other than me, you mean?" He nods ominously.

"Zwicker?"

"No, not Zwicker. Just a couple of kids." He dips the straw carefully into one corner of his milk carton.

"Maybe I wasn't asleep. Maybe I was just thinking."

Still, I could take or leave the sciences. The sciences have two flaws. One, they build from week to week, so if you space out for a few weeks, the train leaves the station and there's no hope of catching up. Two, they rely too much on received wisdom. The reason I haven't done well—and I'm not trying to excuse myself here—is that we were plunked down and expected to memorize the periodic table and all these formulas, and my true question just never got answered. Which is: How do we know all this? How do we know, for instance, that an electron circles around a proton (or whatever), or that carbon consists of five electrons and two protons (or whatever)? Has someone actually seen this with their own eyes? How do we know it isn't all a scam? Had this been answered at the beginning, I may have invested more energy in keeping up.

Now the arts—those are the subjects for me. No building from week to week. You can zone out for days, but as long as you jump back in before the deadline, read the book or look at the painting or listen to the music before that test or discussion, you will get it: the right insight, sometimes a brilliant one, all in a flash. And you don't have to rely on received ideas. You can come up with your own. You can disagree: "No, Ms. Thatcher, I don't think that's what Zora Neale Hurston meant to say." Try pulling that in chemistry!

In the arts, you have a shot at coming up with something new too. While the chances of my discovering or synthesizing a new chemical element are about nil (Billonium? Morrisonium?), my chances of creating a mind-blowing original work are not bad. Even Dad, having dropped out of art school without getting his degree, could pick up his paints one day and do the painting of his career.

I know myself. I will never be well rounded. I will never respond appropriately to meetings in which my guidance counselor tells me I'm not working up to my potential. I will never catch up in chemistry or biology. Instead, I'll focus on music, and a flash of genius will save me. I'll win a songwriting competition sponsored by some organization like ASCAP and find work as a songwriter in Memphis, Austin, or Nashville.

But it's good of Mitchell to watch out for me. We were born on the same day, although he looks sort of middle-aged. He's rotund, and he holds his pants up with suspenders that make him look even rounder. You can't help thinking that although the suspenders were straight when he clipped them on, now they look like the seventy-fifth and hundred fiftieth meridians on a globe.

In English last year, he would signal to me when he thought a poem we were studying contained a coded reference to masturbation. He sat ahead of me and would tilt his head at the appropriate time when one of our classmates read aloud. Andy tried to participate but was never good at it. He picked things that were either too obvious or off the topic, having to do just generally with sex. When we studied Robert Frost, Andy tilted his head at the book title, *You Come Too*.

"How come you guys didn't laugh?" he asked after class.

"Too easy," Mitchell said.

"But what about his horse being queer?"

"That has nothing to do with anything, Andy. The fact that a line makes everyone else in the class laugh doesn't mean it gets a laugh out of me."

The killer came when we were reading "Desiderata" by Max Ehrmann. When Sandi Buscaglia read the last line, "Strive to be happy," I saw the back of Mitch's head tilt very slightly, about five degrees, and I nearly had to leave the room.

Now Gordy drops his lunch bag on the table.

"You know, you were asleep in chemistry class."

"I know."

Mitchell drains his milk and opens a second carton.

"Fortunately," he says, "I took tremendous notes. I can come by with them after school."

The cafeteria noise swells in my ears like a jet engine. I bite into a hard, whitish tomato slice that came with the macaroni. Mitchell waits for me to answer, and I look at Gordy but he doesn't give anything away. I don't want Mitchell at the house right now.

"I notice you haven't invited me over for a while. Are you secretly developing some kind of explosive in your room? Perhaps your ignorance of the difference between hydrogen and helium was just a smokescreen."

"Ha!" Andy says. "That's right, he's developing a bomb."

"Um, no."

"You're writing something, is that it? You spend all your time with the headphones on, opening the door only to accept a tray of food and water."

"Anybody, grapes?" Gordy takes a big bunch from his lunch bag.

Mitchell looks at Gordy. "Our mute friend here tells me you're into New Orleans jazz."

"What I'm really looking into is funeral jazz."

"Okay." Mitchell picks up bits of paper trash and piles

them in one corner of his tray. Normally he can find a way to make anything seem funny or stupid. But even he finds it hard to joke about this. The thing that everyone knows about Gordy, even if they've never spoken to him, is that his mother died right after they moved into town. "Well, could you recommend a couple of titles?"

"Yeah," Andy says. "I'd enjoy listening to some of it." He's doing his earnest Boy Scout thing that Mitchell calls his talking-to-adults voice. Gordy is worse off than I thought. His semi-orphaned state is making him not one of us.

"There's one by the Magnificent Seventh that gives you a good introduction," Gordy says.

"And this is all music that gets played at people's funerals?" Mitchell asks.

"Uh-huh."

Gordy grows even more in my estimation. He's taking the weirdness hit so I don't have to.

TREATMENT REPORT: DAY 10

The pills Dr. Gupta gave Dad have given him what she calls an "atypical dermatological reaction." This sounds much nicer than it looks.

When the rash started out on Dad's abdomen, no one paid much attention. We had gathered around him to wait for improvements, the way a family might pull chairs up to the TV when their favorite show is about to start. Dr. Gupta said not to be too impatient, because the medicine might not completely kick in for weeks. Dad stopped pacing and whistling for a day or two, and it seemed like he might be ready to go back to work.

But then the sores spread to his arms and face, and Linda and I made sickened expressions behind his back. Mom even told him to stop looking in the mirror.

I felt bad that I couldn't deal with the rash.

But one thing I've always liked about myself is that I know my limitations.

SENSITIVITY

The doorbell rings and it's June. Not the month of June, but June from Dad's office.

"Who is it?" Dad calls from his bedroom.

"It's June!" Mom and June sing simultaneously. Then they giggle and hug one another. June rubs Mom's back. "Aw, honey," she says. "How are *you* doing?"

"It's tough," Mom whispers. "He's having trouble with the medication."

"It takes time," June responds, squeezing Mom's hand. "I've heard that sometimes you have to try two or three before you get the right one."

June is a type of woman that usually disturbs Mom. "She treats herself well, doesn't she?" Mom sometimes says, hinting that this may not be a good thing. But she makes an exception when it comes to June. June is wearing a warm-up suit that makes me think of creamy, shampooed sheep. The style of her white-blond hair is practically TV quality.

Dad comes into the living room. June lays a paper cone of carnations and a stack of magazines on the coffee table.

"Ah, *Newsweek*," Dad says.

"I know you like to keep up with the news, Bill," June says.

Dad sits on the couch. I help him roll down his sleeves, careful not to break any of the blisters. "I'm depressed, June," he says. He stares at the floor.

June pats him on the knee. "I hear ya," she says.

Mom, June, and I sit with Dad in the conversation area. Linda is out with her obnoxious friend Jodie. At first June doesn't seem to register that Dad is covered with pink bumps that have grown together to form crests, with rivers of yellow pus running in the valleys. She begins a series of funny stories. One about the people in their office, where she is the bookkeeper. One about the company tennis tournament that Dad sometimes plays in. A couple about her husband, Ben, whom she once considered divorcing but now won't, and about her daughter's bat mitzvah eight months from now, which we are all invited to. Mom goes into the kitchen and gets a tray of chips, salsa, and ginger ale.

"So what's this rash about, Bill?" June asks, leaning across the coffee table. I can't believe she treats Dad's condition so casually. Just an annoyance, like the caterer who wants to serve mini-crepes instead of make-your-own tacos at Lisa's bat mitzvah.

Dad opens his collar, showing June a set of pustules that form, if you look at them from the side, the letter *D*. June bends over the coffee table to inspect, and I can smell her scent of expensive lotions. I, too, have always liked June, or as I call her, Mrs. Melman. I seem to run into her all over town, with no bad repercussions. Once she came into a magazine store and found Mitchell and me looking at what he called "the naked magazines." Mitchell, in fact, was trying to stash a rolled-up one under his sweater. When Mrs. Melman saw us, she said, "There are many good books on that subject at the library," and I never heard anything from Mom about it, which means Mrs. Melman never told.

"They make him look young again, don't they, Adele?" June says to Mom. "Like an oily-faced teenager. Remember acne? Lisa's starting to break out now. She thinks it's the end of the world, but it's not, is it? I told her to think of it as a signal that she's growing up. She thinks she's the center of the universe, you know. I had to tell her, 'You're a lovely girl, honey, and Daddy and I think you're the most beautiful thing on earth, but you have to realize that at this age not everyone is thinking about you all the time like you're thinking about yourself. They're all thinking about themselves.' Right, Billy? Anyway, Bill, I could stop by again with some more magazines and a few of the tubes of little creams Dr. Favola gave Lisa, and you could have fun with them, try them all out. I don't know if they'd have much effect, but we have so many left over because Lisa wants to try them all. She and her friends. I tell her, 'Stop worrying about it, Lisa. You're a beautiful girl, and when you get to be my age you'll be grateful that you had a little extra oil on your skin.' Right, Adele? Is Linda getting to be like that too?"

"Oh, June," Mom sighs. "I wish Linda were a little *less* sure of herself. She hasn't found a thing wrong—not yet, anyway. She keeps staring at herself in the mirror, and she's even given herself a new nickname: Lucky Linda."

"I certainly didn't think of myself as lucky at that age," June answers. "Did you, Adele?"

"Not lucky. Yucky." They both laugh and sip ginger ale.

"Well," June sighs, "most of us are somewhere between lucky and yucky. And I think that's a fine place to be." Mrs. Melman is downplaying her own fantastic beauty. I grab a handful of tortilla chips so I can get the delicate fragrance of her lotions out of my nose.

"I hadn't seen the house next door for a while," June says. "Big, isn't it?"

"Isn't it tacky? People were snickering about it in the supermarket."

June takes a large envelope from her purse and hands it to Dad.

Inside is a card that says, "We heard you were a little under the weather." It shows ten people huddled under a tiny umbrella in driving rain. When Dad opens it to read the signatures, two twenty-dollar bills fall out.

"I tried to stop people from putting money in. I told them it wasn't necessary, but they insisted. Pick up something you really like to eat, or anything that will make you feel more comfortable. I'm sure a number of people would have liked to come in person."

Getting up from the couch, June tugs on the jacket of her warm-up suit. "Thank you for the snacks, sweetie," she says to Mom. She bends down to pat the top of Dad's head, where there are no sores, pecks me on the cheek, and gives Mom a squeeze when Mom opens the door for her. It sounds clichéd, but each of us feels a little special.

Before leaving she looks back at Dad. "Any messages for the poor working stiffs back at the office? Anything you'd like me to report to your fans?"

"Thank them for me, will you, June?" Dad says. He puts a hand up to his neck where his rash is hurting. "Tell them I'll be back soon."

SHRINKAGE

Powerful urges beyond your control. Hospitals, barred windows, white uniforms. Mysterious personality tests that show you black splotches in a butterfly shape. I don't know much about this mental business, but I have to go along for a family visit with Dad's psychotherapist.

I had expected a scientific type in a suit and tie. But when Dr. Fritz stands up to shake hands, saying what a pleasure it is to meet us, he looks like a lumberjack, in a heavy plaid shirt, wool pants, and yellow work boots.

Dr. Fritz leans back in his chair. He looks at each of us for a long time before settling on Dad.

"How are you feeling, Bill?"

Dad doesn't speak right away. Lately he takes a long time choosing his words, as if he has to turn them over first to make sure they're true. He doesn't just throw something out and fix it later, the way healthy people do. And he has plenty to complain about: insomnia and chronic tiredness, loss of appetite and a drop in his weight, seemingly constant worrying, and most of all, not having an interest in the things that used to make life worth living. Even the pacing, hand-rubbing, and whistling, which let up a bit under the blistery meds, have come back. I decide to answer for him.

"Well, he's still not sleeping, if that means anything."

Fritz raises one hand.

"Thanks very much, Billy. I appreciate your trying to help by giving me that information. But right now it's important for me to hear it directly from your dad."

I feel my face burn, at being caught speaking out of turn and also at Fritz's talking-down tone. Fritz is acting like he may have hurt my feelings, so naturally, after a rush of rage and embarrassment, I don't let on that I'm hurt. But still. I thought the point of his occupation was to get you to speak up, not shut up.

"Ha, ha, Billy, you got busted," Linda says.

When Fritz glances at her she covers her mouth.

"Linda, how do you feel about being here, visiting me with your dad?"

"It's no big deal," she says. Her face reddens, and she looks like she's going to pitch a laughing fit. This always happened when we sat next to each other in church. That was the first reason I stopped going.

Don't look at her, I tell myself. *Don't even look at her part of the room.*

"Linda, Billy, if you feel uncomfortable or nervous about being here at first, that's perfectly normal. Over time you'll grow more relaxed when you visit me. The most important thing is that it means a lot to your dad that you're here to support him. I'd like to speak with you more in just a minute, once I've finished checking in with Bill Senior. How are you feeling this week, Bill? No rush. Take as much time as you need to pull your thoughts together."

Mom wants to say something but stops herself. I can tell what she's thinking. That there's so much to say, and our forty-five measly minutes with a qualified individual is slipping away.

"I hated those spots," Dad says finally. "They itched."

Fritz waits for Dad to say more. What a waste of time. After a week and a half with no meds, Dad's rash has flattened out, leaving faded pink lines like capillaries or coral. Looks to me like it's time for a new cure.

"He—," Mom says, and stops there.

Fritz scratches his beard, a full one, not a little beard thing like Dad's.

"Bill, do you think you're ready to try a new medication?"

Good call.

During a long wait, Linda's shoulders begin to shake again. Instead of looking at her, I review all the words I know that begin with *si* and respell them with *psy*—*psygnpost, psyphon, psylo.*

Mom does a dance of annoyance, wiggling her shoulders and head. She taps her necklace (copper discs). Dad told her yesterday that he felt ready to try a new medication, but she isn't about to speak up now. Fritz will have to muddle through without that information. *Psylent treatment.*

"Yeah," Dad says finally. "I'll try it."

"You'll try it?" Fritz repeats.

"I'll give the new medication a shot."

A photo on the wall shows Fritz in a sailboat with a small child. The boat has tilted up and Fritz is leaning out over the water, working the tiller with a huge, avid smile.

Linda stiffens. Fritz has aimed his attention at her. He's staring at her, the same way he stared at Dad.

"How are you holding up during your father's illness, Linda? It must be affecting you a great deal."

Linda is stunned. Not only is Fritz staring at her, Dad is too. *Psyamese. Psymultaneous.* Her face reddens and I think she's going to lose it. Look away, look away.

Everyone waits to hear what Linda has to say.

When I glance back at Linda, she looks somber, like she's being interviewed for the network news.

"Well, of course it bothers me that Dad's sick and everything, but I just try to be there for him. That's what a family's for, isn't it? To take care of each other?"

What a laugh! Linda couldn't take care of a goldfish. All she cares about is doing arts and crafts projects and huddling with her little friend Jodie.

"That's absolutely true," Fritz says. "I like the way you put that, Linda—to take care of each other." He nods five or six times. "And how's Bill Junior doing during this difficult time for the family?"

Oh ho! So *now* he wants me to talk. When it's my turn. When I'm next in line. When my number is called.

"How's school going, for instance?"

"Well . . ." Nobody has asked me this for a while. "It's a little difficult to concentrate, to be honest."

"Mm-hmm, it is difficult to concentrate. But I want to remind you how important it is, especially if this illness goes on for a while, to take care of your life and make sure you can fulfill your own responsibilities. I have a feeling that you are someone who will make a real contribution to the world."

Fritz continues staring while Linda makes a face at me across the room. A professional psychologist thinks I have potential and not Linda! I will lord this over her afterward. Although it would mean a lot more coming from someone who actually knew me.

I can't get over feeling that Fritz doesn't know it's rude to stare at people, and someone should clue him in. I read once that in many cultures, if someone stares at you it means they're either going to kill you or have sex with you, and either way my parents would be deeply annoyed. I have a flash-image of my father leaping over the desk and menacing Fritz with a paperweight, instantly charged into health by the deep instinctive need to protect me.

Fritz then "checks in" with Mom, who repeats a fancier version of Linda's winning formula about the family taking care of each other. It's unusual for her to try this hard to impress someone.

Fritz makes some notations and closes our folder. "In the course of our work together, we may eventually explore some deep emotional issues that will require a great deal of dedication from you, because they will summon painful and difficult feelings. But we're not at that point yet, and I don't see any need to rush. For today we're going to practice some new cognitive strategies, or thought strategies. These strategies are quick and—I don't want to say superficial, but superficial is not such a bad description. The main thing is that they are easy to learn and you can start using them right away. Now slide your chairs closer, right up to my desk, that's it."

We've already improved at staring back at Fritz. The four of us are aligned opposite his desk, achieving a four-on-one group counterstare. I should have mentioned earlier that Fritz is not what you would call handsome. In fact, he resembles a Pekingese dog in a landslide. He has a high forehead and Pekingese-like features that occupy only the lower half of his face and nestle into his beard. The beard blends into his chest and neck hair. Everything on the front of him seems to have slipped down one place. But we're seriously concentrating, not only drinking in but also wringing out every word. When he tilts his face to review a pamphlet on his desk, we tilt our faces too, like four gyroscopes.

He pushes his chair back and shrugs his shoulders to loosen them.

"Okay, everyone, deep breath, in and out. *Mmmmmph-pheeww.*"

Mmmmmph-pheeww.

"Loosen clothing if necessary. Get as comfortable as possible."

We shake out our arms and legs like sprinters preparing for a race, plant our feet flat on the floor.

Fritz links his fingers over his belly. "All of us are plagued by negative self-talk that can create anxiety. This can consist of criticisms, negative fantasies, or recurring thoughts of things we should not have said or done, or painful reminders of things we should have said or done but for some reason did not. Does anyone recognize this tendency in himself or herself? An example, anybody?"

"Hooo," Mom whispers, crossing her legs again. I think she means: so many of them, where to even start?

"Bill Senior?"

Dad moistens his lips but says nothing.

Fritz unclasps his hands and looks receptive.

"Sometimes I'm convinced that I won't be able to go back to work," Dad says softly.

"And what would happen then?"

"Well . . . my family would become indigent."

"That means we would be broke," I explain to Linda.

Fritz ignores me this time. "Very good example, Bill." He nods, a rolling, whole-body nod. "Very good example.

Now when you say this to yourself about not working, you know it's negative self-talk because it makes you feel bad."

We nod.

"And the second part of that thought, the part about being indigent, is going to make you feel even worse. So your goal with this technique is to stop the thought as soon as it starts, before you even get to the second part. And you're going to do that by saying these words to that inner voice in your head: 'Cancel, cancel!'"

Murmuring: "Cancel, cancel." We're still nodding.

"And there's a picture, a visual, you can add to it too. While you're saying 'Cancel, cancel,' you can picture yourself drawing an X through the thought, or stamping it out with one of those red circles with the diagonal through it."

"Like the No Smoking symbol."

"Exactly, Linda. Or conjure up your own picture. Whatever works best for you."

"You know, that's very good," Mom says. And she mouths the words to herself: *Cancel, cancel.*

Fritz rests his elbows on the desk. "Challenge yourself to say 'Cancel, cancel' as quickly as possible. Right on the heels of the negative thought. Make a game of it. Because the less time the thought spends in your mind, the less it will affect your mood and contribute to a downward spiral. Ready to try it?"

Dad seems pretty caught up in this, more involved than he's been in a while.

"Here we go. I'm going to lose my job and—"

"Cancel, cancel," we blurt out.

"I'm going to—"

"Cancelcancel." Three of us are speed-talking, with Dad trailing behind.

"I'm—"

"Cancelcancel."

"Okay." Fritz raises both hands over his head. "Ho!" He laughs in booming, individual cannonball shots. "I'm a negative thought, and I just gave up. You can't get much faster than that. Very good work. Let's relax and breathe for a moment."

Mmmmmph-pheeww.

"Who's ready for another one? You all are. Since you're doing so well, I'm going to give you an opposite, or complementary, strategy to the one you just learned. This one is to reinforce any *positive* self-talk that runs through your mind. Say I observe to myself, 'I've had a terrific day.' I want that thought to hang around for a while. So, to encourage it to stick around, I say, 'Welcome!' To confirm and validate that positive thought: 'Welcome!' And you can add a mental image of this gesture."

Fritz has struck an openhanded pose, like someone catching rain after a drought.

"Welcome!" we mutter, practicing the gesture.

"I am a useful and worthwhile person," Fritz says.

"Welcome!"

Fritz checks the clock on the wall. "We're done for today. I know you've all worked really hard in this session, especially you, Bill. And I have to compliment you. You and Adele have a lovely family."

"Thank you," Mom says, walking to the door.

"Welcome!"

"How did you like your first session, kids?" Mom asks while she unlocks the car.

"Well, I learned something. We're all supposed to take care of each other!"

"Cut it out," Linda says.

"Don't make fun of the doctor, Billy," Mom says. "Your father feels comfortable with him."

"I'm not making fun of the doctor. I'm making fun of you!"

"That's enough, Billy," Dad says.

It's hard to argue with him right now.

ON THE MALL ROAD

A group of men in heavy parkas cluster by a bench on our main street.

"I like your light!" one calls in accented English. The others guffaw. Well, you can't pay much attention to stupid comments. A headlight is practical when you do a lot of night riding. If they find me foolish, so be it. Some of the immigrants in town ride bikes too, but I get the impression it's because they can't afford cars yet, and as soon as they can buy a nice pickup it will be *adios, bicicleta*.

Everyone's in a rush to get a driver's license, but I'm in no hurry to get a car. You know those old movies, British mysteries or French classics, where you see a guy riding a bike in a tweed jacket and tie? That's very classy. Except that in the U.S. you would have to wear a helmet, which ruins the look.

Why hasn't anyone done a movie about a group of bicyclists? It would open with kind of a skittery theme on an electric fiddle, which gets louder as a dozen classic bikes appear, another dozen, forty in all. They burst into stunts: ramp jumps and wheelies. The scene looks like pandemonium but has been drilled to clockwork precision. It could be the story of outlaw bikers taking midnight rides on hacked bikes that defy safety laws, or musicians who work as bike messengers by day. Or an action movie about rival gangs, loaded with street-fighting scenes. I can picture the movie poster: "Spokes. What goes around comes around." A closeup of a guy's face through the wheel he's repairing. His eye is circled with a gang tattoo.

Maybe if Dad rode a bike again, like he did as a kid, he could get his old energy back. It could be that easy: tire himself during the day, sleep better at night, and we all go back to normal. Maybe, maybe, maybe. I try not to think about it too much. But Mom and the doctors have to keep trying. If they weren't saying maybe, maybe, maybe they would just sit around asking why, why, why. As in a traditional blues song. Something like:

Why does a man feel tired
Why does a man feel dead

When something something something
And the something in his head

It's a world of trouble, baby
Oh Mister Trouble, let me go
Get your something from my something
And leave me to my—

Studio? Radio?

I should be able to plug in that rhyme. I don't want to use a rhyming dictionary unless I'm absolutely, definitely stuck.

"Hey, Bicycle Boy!"

At the red light I feel something wet across my eyes and cheeks. Not blood? A Ford Explorer screeches forward, bolting from me as soon as the light turns green. Guys in the car are laughing, and one turns back to taunt me, holding a bottle out the window.

I pull the bike over to the curb and press my hand against my face. My heart is slamming. No, not blood. Something cool and clear. I sniff. Probably just water. He squirted me with a bottle of water. Could be worse. Could be bleach. Or urine.

Who would do a thing like that?

Probably frat boys from Hawthorne State, looking for a cheap laugh. If so, is there something about me that provoked this? Were they cruising for victims, or did my appearance make them want to humiliate me? Are they threatened by my challenge to automotive dominance?

Christ, I wish I had had something to throw into their car. Or at least that I recovered in time to say something back. "Bicycle Boy." Really clever. Really humiliating. That put me in my place, all right. Oh my gosh, you're right, I am riding a bike! Thanks for pointing that out, I hadn't realized it! And now I realize how socially unacceptable that is! Idiot me! It's four wheels from now on!

Or was the "boy" part the big insult? Crap, I'm only fifteen! That makes me unfit to live! If only I could be a college guy like you, with nothing to do but drive around soaking people!

Now, what was I just thinking about?

Still, it could be worse. Awful things. Like bleach, right in the eyes. Or, I heard of somebody riding along when a car passenger smashed a glass bottle in front of him, probably hoping that broken glass would fly up into the cyclist's face. Or girls getting their rear ends grabbed. You could fall right into traffic after something like that. Why can't people just get along?

What could you say to those guys? "Bicycle Boy." Why is that so clever? Is it the repetition of the *b* at the beginning of both words (i.e., alliteration) that they think is devastating? If so, would they be devastated if I alliterated them back? College Clowns? Water-Wielding Wusses?

Explorer . . . Excrementheads? But that's the thing about these incidents. You dwell on them too long, and you never do recoup. You think you'll get your own back, but you can't. It eats away at you. They've got you either way.

Okay, now I've completely lost my train of thought.

TREATMENT REPORT: DAY 27

Dad has started a new med. Now, in addition to being worried, tired, malnourished, and sleep-deprived, his fear level seems to be rising. He looks like he would jump at the sight of a Fauvist painting. And once I saw his hand shake when he drank a glass of water.

I don't know if the pills are causing this or if Dad is simply getting worse, but I suspect the pills are at fault. If so, maybe Dr. Gupta attended the medical school at Paradox College, where in addition to learning things like (1) You have to be cruel to be kind, and (2) If you love something, let it go, she also learned (3) To calm someone down, scare them.

Of course, I don't know anything. Most likely Dad is 100 percent on track for where he needs to be.

THE SHORTEST DAY

At six p.m., it's already been dark for two hours. A thin layer of mixed rain and snow has come down, leaving the road tacky and hissing. After dinner we settle into the conversation area with Dad's brother Marty and watch the tree blink. Marty brought his camcorder so he can film us opening our gifts. He shoots Mom placing a turkey leg on a plate beside Dad's chair.

"He might want to pick at that," she says.

Marty pans across the cards strung on ribbons above the fireplace, a combination of Merry Christmas and Get Well. Dad's office has sent a fruit basket wrapped in gold cellophane, with a note saying "An apple a day keeps the doctor away!"

"Gee, that's easy," Linda said when she accepted the basket from the deliveryman. "Do they think he's suffering from irregularity?"

Marty sits beside Dad and rests his arm along the

back of the couch. He was recently separated from Aunt Stephanie, who was, as Mom and Dad always said, a keeper. She traveled all over the world setting up computer systems for a big hotel chain. When she left Uncle Marty and took Marty Junior, the new baby cousin we never met, we couldn't help feeling, as a family, that she was just too good for us.

Now Marty always dresses as if he's out on a date. Pressed jeans, smooth mustache, styled hair. But he's getting that defeated look some divorced fathers have. The look that says they used to be part of something.

The phone rings in the kitchen. "That must be Sally and Adam," Mom says, jumping up. There's no telling when she'll be back once she starts yakking with her sister.

"Go sit under the tree, Linda," Marty says, hoisting the camera onto his shoulder. Linda poses like a little kid waiting for Santa. She's wearing a long pioneer skirt and a snowman sweater of Grandma Pearl's that she found in the attic.

It's odd having Christmas Eve without music. Normally Mom would be playing a Nat King Cole Christmas CD that someone copied for her, but out of respect for Dad, we're chestnut free. Marty begins to hum.

"Well? Can you make it?" Mom asks on the phone. "Why not? Well, what other plans? I thought you were coming *here*. I never told you we didn't feel up to company. We do feel up to company, very much so. We would have loved more company this year. I made cookies and eggnog and everything. Marty's here. No, just Marty. Well, do you want to drop the kids off here and I'll bring them back later? *Sally* . . ." Mom's voice sounds like it's wearing off. She takes a deep breath, the way the therapist told us to.

"Adele? Is everything okay?" Dad asks.

"Yes, fine." Mom puts her hand over the phone and steps into the living room. "They're not coming."

"Yes," she says into the phone, "Bill received a box from you. He hasn't opened it yet. But he looks very pleased. Actually, to be honest, he doesn't look pleased, but if he were feeling better, I know he'd be extremely gratified to get the package. Call me tomorrow? What time? Okay. Merry Christmas. Yes, you too, 'bye."

"Excuse me a minute." Mom goes from the kitchen into the hall. She's rushing, almost like she has to go to the bathroom. She disappears for a while.

"Do you want to see what I got you?" Marty asks.

"We better wait for Mom to come back," Linda says. She sorts the skimpy stash of presents, reading the name labels and tossing them into piles under the tree. She bumps a branch that holds an ornament with small sleigh bells. The bells jingle, and Dad winces.

"Sorry," she says without looking at him.

Marty fiddles with the camera and hums to himself. Before the illness, Dad spent hours consoling Marty and giving him advice about the separation. Now it seems like Marty's trying to put a holiday face on and not mention his heartbreak.

"Well," Linda says, "this is shaping up to be a Christmas for the record books, isn't it? At least Aunt Stephanie used to bring us decent presents."

I crawl across the floor and drape tinsel on her head. "Cancel, cancel, Linda!"

"That's perfect, kids," Marty says. "Do that again."

Mom comes back, wiping her eyes and looking furious. "Who wants a cookie?" she commands, passing a plastic tray in the shape of a bell. Marty and I each take a couple of cookies. Dad takes one and promptly forgets about it, leaving it on the arm of his chair like a business card or other inedible.

Linda places an oversize box on Dad's lap. "Here's your present from Sally and Adam. Watch out, it's a heavy one."

Marty sets up a shot over Dad's shoulder. "Three, two, one, action!"

"I might need help opening this," says Dad. "It's taped up pretty tight."

I crawl to the couch, feeling like a kid again, and sit next to Dad. I cut the brown paper flaps with my pocket knife. Inside is a corrugated cardboard box.

"Smile again, Billy," says Uncle Marty. "You're helping your dad, huh?"

"Yep."

"I hope they didn't get you anything too expensive," Mom says. "I told them we were keeping it simple this year. I wasn't even expecting to exchange with them."

"It's a fisherman's trophy of some kind," Dad says. "A bass. Why would they send me this?"

"Isn't that handsome?" says Marty from behind the camera.

A large stuffed fish is attached to a wooden plaque. Pulling away the last piece of tissue, I see a switch on the plaque and turn it on. The fish twists its head and tail and begins to sing.

Here's a little song I wrote
You might want to sing it note for note
Don't worry, be happy
In every life we have some trouble
When you worry you make it double
Don't worry, be happy

Dad covers his face with the box lid. "How horrible! Turn it off, Billy, turn it off!"

"It's just a toy, Dad. See?"

Marty drops his camera. "Are you all right, bro? It's okay. It's okay. It's over."

"I can't believe it!" Mom says. "I can't believe they would send a grotesque gift like that instead of showing up. It's so insensitive. Good God, Sally."

"I like it," Linda says. "Can I have it? I'll play it in my room, very quietly."

"Here," Dad says, "you keep it." His hands are shaking.

Linda takes the present to her room, laughing at me over her shoulder as if we had been competing for this piece of musical taxidermy. Sometimes I wonder if Linda would even know what she wanted if I weren't around.

"I can't believe Sally couldn't make it," Mom says, biting into a cookie. "Or didn't want to make it. Do you know this is our first Christmas apart?"

"Shhh, Adele," Dad says. "Don't even think about it."

"Okay, now," Marty says. "Ready for your close-ups. One at a time."

"You're going to leave the camera on, Uncle Marty?" Linda asks when she comes back. "What if Dad gets something else that's freakish?"

"It's fine, Linda," Mom says. "Have fun with it, Marty."

Mom had announced that we should keep our gift buying fairly simple this Christmas. Now we go around the room opening one present apiece, expressing more fake delight than usual. It's hard to know whose benefit this is for—Dad's, Mom's, Marty's, or the camera's. Dad is the only person who isn't playacting, although he tries to say something appreciative each time. It must be good for him to keep busy—even with the bass incident, he hasn't had to get up and pace. Marty has given Linda a handheld video game console, Mom a personal digital assistant, and me a fancy electronic odometer I'll never use.

"Cool!" Linda shouts, winding her face into a grimace

that she'll be embarrassed about five years from now.

"I haven't got your gift yet, Bill," Marty tells Dad. "I need a little more time. I wanted it to be really, really special."

Linda made friendship bracelets for everyone—plain ones for the men and a daisy-patterned one for Mom. I bought a small box of oil paints for Dad, soap for Mom, and socks for Linda. Nothing for Marty because I didn't know he was going to be here. "Don't give it another thought, buddy," Marty says. "You're good to me all year round, right?" Mom gives each person thermal underwear and a box of hard candy.

"Now it's time for your father's presents," Mom says.

"You had time to shop, Dad?" Linda asks. "You didn't have to get us anything."

"Not exactly," Mom says. She takes a handful of small envelopes from the top of the brick room divider and gives one to Marty, Linda, and me, and takes one for herself. "Let's open them all at once," she says.

Inside the envelopes are note cards saying

WHEN I AM WELL

I WILL TAKE YOU

Mine says "to the Museum of Fine Arts." Linda's says "on the Swan Boats." Mom's says "to the North End." Marty's says "to Fenway Park."

"Fun!" Linda shouts.

"God, bro, that's so nice. I can't wait."

"Adele helped me with them."

Marty's chin begins to shake. "It's been such a tough year, with the separation and everything. You've been amazing. Everyone else got sick of hearing about it."

"There goes another one," Linda says.

"Excuse me," Marty says. He goes to the hall bathroom, flushing the toilet as soon as he gets inside.

"I guess that's it, then," Mom says, taking the big tray of cookies back to the kitchen.

Linda and I collect the wrapping paper and stuff it into bags. When Marty comes back, he takes Dad by the elbow.

"Let's go for a walk, bro," he says, walking him to the coat closet. "We'll stroll up and down the street and see everybody's decorations. Let's get you good and bundled up."

Once they leave, Mom retrieves the turkey leg from beside the armchair and wraps it in foil. She turns off the room lights. Only the tree is still glowing.

"That wasn't such a bad Christmas," she says.

FRITZ SAYS

Fritz says:

"It's important for you to feel as functional and normal as possible while this is going on. So shower each day. Get dressed right away, as soon as you get out of bed—don't sit around in your pajamas. Get some exercise daily, even a twenty-minute walk or some calisthenics, sit-ups, and mild push-ups in the living room. Be sure to eat something, especially protein. Even if it doesn't taste good, just get it down. Okay?"

Fritz says:

"I realize that you're just trying to help, and I appreciate that. You're very good people, and I value your thoughts and ideas. But it's important not to interrupt. Although I really am treating you as a family to some extent, I'd like to keep your husband and father as the focus. So I'd like you to try, even though I know it feels difficult, to hold back a little bit . . . in fact, quite a bit. Thank you. Let's try that again, okay?"

Fritz says:

"Let's see if we can work out some really effective techniques for helping Bill be able to answer the questions in his own way, in his own time. Now, let me model for you how I ask Bill a question and wait for his answer. I ask my question; then I keep looking right into his eyes—see the direct line from my eyes to his—and I wait calmly and patiently while he formulates his answer. I might even be willing to wait five minutes if I have to. Why not? What's to lose if I do? What I really don't want to do is to squelch his answer in any way. He tends to speak very quietly right now, so I don't want the relative loudness of my own voice to drown out his answer. He's also speaking rather slowly, so I wouldn't want the relative quickness of my voice to beat him to the punch and perhaps drive his own answer right out of his head. Once he does begin to speak, I'll listen receptively until I'm sure he's finished. So could all of us take turns trying that?"

HOWL

Someone in the house is shouting.

It's Dad who's shouting. An intruder has broken into our house. An intruder is trying to kill Dad.

I sit up in bed. My body runs alongside my heart, trying to jump on.

I feel for my bike frame and grab the tire pump. It's light but would deliver a solid blow.

The lights are on in Mom and Dad's room. Dad's eyes are shut. Every time he shouts, his head rises off the pillow. Mom kneels on the floor beside him, shaking his arm.

"Wake up, Bill! Wake up! Bill! Stop it!"

"What's wrong with him?"

Linda runs in from the hall, wearing sweatpants and a T-shirt.

Dad shouts again.

Linda shouts back, sounding just like Dad. They're not

shouting words. It's a preword and I don't know where they learned it.

"Linda! Stop it!" Mom says.

"Mom! Why is he doing this?"

"I don't know, Billy. He just is. He just started shouting like this."

"Why don't you make him stop it?"

"I can't!"

Linda looks into the hall, hopping up and down. "Where's Dad? He'll know what to do! I'm going to go get Dad!"

Mom grabs her by the shoulders. "Linda! *Linda!* What are you talking about? This is Dad. He's already here. He's the one who's yelling."

"Oh! He's already here. I forgot." She starts to cry and leans on Mom.

"Linda, you have to calm down. You have to help me."

"But I'm afraid!"

"I can't wake him up. Somebody try something!"

"Come on, Dad," I urge. My voice leaves my throat in shreds like splinters. "You can do it. You can wake up."

I really don't know if he can. What if he can't?

I drop the pump and climb across the bed to shake him. How long has it been since I've crawled into my parents' bed—ten years? Back then it was a tract, a room to itself.

"Come on, wake up. It's not real. If you wake up, you won't be scared anymore."

"In another minute," Mom says, "I'm calling an ambulance."

"Dad, stop," Linda says. "Please stop, okay? Please wake up. You're scaring me. Okay. Okay." She breathes deep the way the doctor told us to, but each breath has a rattle in it like she's swallowed cellophane. "I know. Let's pry his eyes open."

Bending over him with one fingertip, she slides up his eyelids. He's still shouting without looking at us, in a separate world that we can't get to.

Then Dad's irises contract.

"He's awake," Linda says.

I press Dad's arm. His pajama shirt is soaked. "Dad, it was just a nightmare. Come on. Sit up. Sit up."

"He's awake, Mom. Dad, it's okay," Linda says. "You're home in bed."

"All right."

"You're home. You were having a nightmare."

"Was I? My God." Dad's voice is rough, like that night in the kitchen.

Linda and I surround Dad, but Mom stays back. Dad's nightmare must have scared her. She looks like someone who walks along the edge of a pool not knowing what they'll find. A koi, a piranha, a dead body, their own reflection.

"Are you going to be all right, Bill? I was just about to call an ambulance."

"Maybe he should keep sitting up, Mom. Keep sitting up. You'd better stay awake for a while, until you're sure it's gone away."

"I'm awake. I'm awake."

Linda tugs the corner of his pillow. "I'm the one who woke you up, Dad."

"Thank you, honey." He feels for her hand, squeezes it. "When you saw me, you were all right."

"What was this nightmare?" I ask. "It must have been a whopper."

"What was it, Dad?" Linda echoes. "Was it pretty scary?"

"I was alone. . . ."

Crawling back to Mom's side of the bed, I settle against the headboard. "So, you were alone?"

"That's right. I was sealed up in a metal box . . . with a window in it."

"Mom," Linda asks, "can I turn on all the lights so we feel less nervous?"

"If it will make you feel better."

"Don't say anything important till I get back."

Lights come on in rooms, shaping our box of life beside the highway. The drivers on 128 may notice a lit-up house, but they know nothing about Dad's nightmare. Probably no other family is awake in this section of Hawthorne.

"What do you think the metal box was?" The obvious thought is a coffin, but I hope he'll say "phone booth" and break this mood.

"It was like a submarine, because I was dropped into the ocean. But nobody knew that I was inside. First it was bobbing on the surface. Then it started to sink. I could see the water through the window."

Dad links his phrases slowly, but we listen without interrupting, as the doctor said we should. I try to picture the dream, picture myself in it. I feel that if I get it right, just the way Dad dreamed it, the spell will break and it won't bother him again.

"I wanted to get out, and I knew it had a door in it when I first went inside, but when the box began to sink the door had disappeared."

"Why were you inside it in the first place?" Linda asks.

"Does that really make any difference, Linda?" Mom asks.

"I'm trying to figure out what it means."

"It doesn't mean anything. Don't you see what the problem is? It's those pills they've got him on."

"That's what it must be," Dad says. "Those pills."

Of course. "Well, that's good then, isn't it?" I comment.

"How is it good?"

It's good because Dad is not really in a metal box that's sinking.

Mom finds a clean pajama top in a pile of folded laundry on the dresser. She holds it out to Dad while he takes off the soaked one. "I could kick myself. How could I let you take anything without looking into it more closely?"

"Dad," Linda asks, "do you think that if you had stayed asleep, you eventually would have found a way out of the box?"

"I don't think we need to know any more about this," Mom answers without looking at Linda. "It doesn't matter what the nightmare means, it's just bad enough that it happened. Try to get it out of your mind, Bill. Do you want to read something?"

"Maybe we should have made the decision together," Dad says, buttoning the new shirt.

"Together? Bill—" It seems like Mom wants to say that Dad hasn't been able to decide anything for at least a month now. But how can she tell him this? No one ever actually says to him that he's anything less than normal. "Well, do you mean you didn't want the pills? If we had decided together, would you have not gone ahead with it? Do you want to go off them?"

"I didn't want them. I knew they wouldn't help." Dad suddenly seems more wise instead of less, like his dream packed him something to carry back to the rest of us. His calmness spooks me, and I wish there were more lights for Linda to turn on.

"Why didn't you say something at the time?" Mom asks. "Why didn't you refuse to take them?"

"Because you seemed so happy."

"You were making me happy?" Mom is still holding the sweaty pajama top. "You took them to make me happy? But I did think it was going to help. Something had to."

"Are you all right, then, Dad?" I ask. "Can we go back to bed now?" I was thinking of getting up extra early. I have an oral report to give tomorrow, and I haven't even started it yet. I feel like my blood has slowed down finally. A section of my face, right between my eyebrows, had actually been jumping.

"I don't feel like sleeping," Linda says. "Dad, do you want to sit up for the rest of the night with the lights on and watch TV? There might be an old movie on. Then when the movie's over, I'll make pancakes."

"That's all right, honey. Your mother and I will sit up for a few minutes and talk. Oh, God."

"I'm going to bed. Maybe you should move into a different room," I suggest. "To just, you know, forget things. Remove the reminders or whatever. Maybe you should sleep on the couch tonight."

"He'll be all right," Mom says. "But I vote with Linda. Anyone who wants to can leave their lights on."

DAD, HOW CAN YOU GO TO CALIFORNIA?

That same night I have my own dream, that an airline introduced a special reduced airfare from Boston to California. In my dream, the fare was extremely cheap— $142 round-trip—because of the volume of passengers that could be conveyed on a single plane. Each passenger's head, you see, was separated from the body and sealed in a plastic bag. The body was maintained at home with intravenous feeding until the "extra-value passenger" (the head) returned.

Dad's head went to California in a plastic bag, stacked as palletized cargo in a freight compartment with the heads of other budget travelers, most of whom were traveling for business. They would be able to do all the necessary negotiating and communicating in this compact state. Who needed a body to attend a meeting?

But after Dad's head had been away for several days, it struck me that he might be in jeopardy. I rushed into his room to find his body seated upright in a special chair, wearing white hospital pajamas. His systems were hooked up, his blood was pumping, his chest moved in and out. The only bad sign was that his skin looked shiny and goldish. *But how,* I shouted in my sleep, *could we have let him go to California?* If his head were somehow diverted, like a piece of lost luggage, we would never be able to put him together again.

In the dream I stayed for a week beside his body, always awake, watching every rise and fall of his chest, waiting for his head to come back—across the country, through the dollies, trolleys, hand trucks, and conveyors of Logan Airport, back home to us.

A NOTE TO THE READER

Oh, I know you can never walk a mile in my worn-out bedroom slippers.

But can you see how important all this is?

I want you to see it.

So you will know what was lost.

So you'll never think, while reading this, that I tried to do too much.

BULWARK

"Dr. Fritz, please. Adele Morrison. No, I can't wait. No, I can't hold. I don't care, I need to talk to him *right now*. How long? Tell me specifically how long I have to wait. How many minutes? All right, but no longer."

Mom holds on to the phone, watching Dad. Dad's at the table in his pajamas, breaking a Pop-Tart into small pieces. I finish my cereal and put my breakfast dishes in the sink before Mom starts to speak again.

"Dr. Fritz, the medication you've started us on . . . No, it's not a good morning. No, I'm not going to tell you how I am, and I'm not going to ask how you are. The medication you and Dr. Gupta prescribed for my husband is completely unacceptable. He began shouting in his sleep last night and frightened our children. My daughter was completely terrified, and I almost called an ambulance. . . . Yes, he was shouting. He was having nightmares. Extremely bad ones, apparently, from the sound of it. I had difficulty waking him. All of us are rattled by the experience. . . . Well, your questions are certainly very impressive-sounding, but to return to my original point without getting bogged down in specifics: This medication is unacceptable. . . . Oh, this nightmare thing is uncommon? Well, that changes the situation, doesn't it? What do we care how uncommon it is if it happens to us?

"No, I'm not willing to 'wait it out.' . . . I don't think we can afford to wait another two weeks for him to adjust. If this is what it's like, we're not going to wait two days, or even two minutes. Here are your choices: You and Dr. Gupta can switch him to something different *today*, and it has to be more effective than what you've given him so far, or you can try to cure him without medication. Which is it?"

Mom listens to Fritz while watching Dad put an edge of Pop-Tart crust in his mouth. Her cheeks are full of air, like she's saying a word that starts with *B*. She puts the receiver back on the wall without saying good-bye to Fritz.

Mom leans against the kitchen counter, her eyes avoiding Dad's chair. "He says he'll discuss it with me at the next appointment."

PSYONARA

Mom says the medical establishment has let her down again. She's entirely disillusioned with Fritz. He's fallen off his pedestal. Mom says that Fritz never really cared about helping Dad. He only took the case to help pay for his sailboat.

TREATMENT REPORT: DAY 41

Mom and Dad stay home at the time of the next scheduled appointment with Fritz.

The phone rings and rings.

part two

COMPOSED IN A CHEMISTRY NOTEBOOK

"The Happy Pills"
(Sung by a chorus of doctors)

The white one just might help you,
Though it makes your heart beat fast
And it makes your tongue feel sandy
And your eyes feel hard as glass.
So there's clanging in your left ear
And a buzzing in your right—
If you overlook the symptoms
It will help you sleep all night.
Tra-la!

Or you could try the blue one,
If you don't care how you look,
If you don't mind tiny blisters
Filled with icky greenish gook

That will start out on your stomach
And then overrun your skin.
Anyway, you don't get out much—
So you won't mind staying in.
Tra-la!

This new one's just the ticket.
Just ignore the gloomy press.
Those stories are all nonsense
Placed by nuts seeking redress.
Yes, one patient shot his family,
But that doesn't happen much—
We know other patients like it,
And that's good enough for us.
Tra-la!

This red one is a killer.
You'll feel like a brand-new man,
If you don't mind weird sensations
In your procreative gland.
Call my cell phone if it stiffens
And you can't get it to bend—
You'll be rushed back with a siren

And you'll never shtup again.
Tra-la!

Tra-la, la, la, la!
That will be one hundred twenty-five dollars, please.

"Oh, that's funny, Billy," Mom says.

TRICK OR TREATMENT

"Your father and I have just finished discussing his options," Mom says. "We feel fortunate to have skirted what was obviously a medical disaster in the making."

Uncle Marty talked Dad into watching a college basketball game with him in the den. From the other end of the house we can hear Marty shouting. He has a bundle of money on the game.

"At this point we're going to change our strategy. We're going to do what I initially thought we should have done, and that is to care for him on our own. From this point your father is going medication free, and his symptoms, including the bizarre sleep disturbance, will have a chance to subside.

"Our home routines will be different for a while. I spoke to Dad's office and they're extending his medical leave. We expect it won't be a long one once he recovers from the medications. I'm going to change my work schedule"—

Mom's voice breaks, and she stares at Triumph until she's calm again—"to half-time, from two thirty in the afternoon until six. That will allow us to provide Dad with continuous care throughout the day. Billy, you will come home directly after school so that you can take over from me at two fifteen. It would be best if you and I can overlap for a few minutes before I leave, in case there's anything we need to go over.

"I know how scary it's been for both of you to see him this way. He told me he hates to have you see him like this. He never wanted to be someone you felt sorry for. He wanted to be someone you looked up to. He wouldn't even want me to have this conversation with you. He wouldn't even want me to tell you what I just said. But I did, so there it is.

"Your father and I are going to need all your help to get through this time. Once it's over . . . we'll turn the page on this chapter and never look back again. What do you think about that?"

Linda is flopped on my bed. "Of course, Mom," she says. "We'll do whatever it takes to get Dad well again."

Mom raises her eyebrows at me.

I raise my eyebrows back.

"You can go, Linda."

"Okay, Mom." She kisses Mom on the way out.

Mom stays in my desk chair. I'm down low this time in the beanbag.

"What?" she asks, looking down at me.

"I know you need me and everything."

"Yes."

"But—I'm coming home right after school?"

"Yes."

"And staying here until six o'clock? Monday through Friday?"

"That's right."

"What about Linda?"

"What about her?"

"Shouldn't she come right home too?"

Mom has a few ways of looking at people that make them shut up. One is to remove her reading glasses and place them on top of her head. She kind of combs the arm of the glasses slowly through her hair first in a way that can be scary. But this time it doesn't work.

"Shouldn't she?"

Mom shrugs.

"You're not going to answer me?"

"You know she wants to help. But she can't, really. She's just too young. This is not the time to complain."

"Shouldn't she get a chance to try? Maybe she'd turn out to be good at it. Better than me, even."

"Billy."

"Maybe she has a knack, or a special gift."

"Will you keep your voice down, please?"

"Hey, I know."

"What?"

"You could get her a little nurse's uniform. Wouldn't she look adorable in it?"

"What is the matter with you? This isn't the time."

What is the precisely calibrated bored look that says Mom's judgment is so obviously wrong that everyone realizes it except her?

"What if I want to do something after school?"

"You have important plans?"

"That's neither here nor there. What if I did have them?"

"This isn't forever. It's just for a few weeks. Until he's over it."

"What if I say no?"

"I'm not giving you a choice."

"All right, then, I guess I won't say no."

"It's only for a few weeks."

"A few weeks. All right."

After Mom leaves, I take her spot at the desk. Inside the desk is a Hohner Special 20 harmonica Grandma Pearl got me. I had asked for it, in fact, but it's still sealed in the package with the instruction book. Had I ever learned to play it, I would create an ugly sound at a special decibel level only Mom could hear, letting her know I will never be her orderly.

BATTLESHIP

I've been playing Battleship with Dad. Somehow, he always ends up looking for my Destroyer last.

The Destroyer is the very smallest of five boats—it occupies only two spaces on the game board—and so it can be hidden anywhere. Dad seems to have guessed a hundred times, systematically, all over the board. In fact, he seems to be creating a scientific net of guesses to throw over the grid and ensnare my Destroyer. I can see his web of guesses spreading over the grid, from A1 way up in the lefthand corner, seeping downward and outward over the transparent green plastic of my ocean and covering the four boats of mine that he has already sunk.

Yet somehow he's missed D9.

In the meantime I'm just as systematically trying to avoid sinking his last boat, the massive, five-space Aircraft Carrier. I'm doing a kind of hot-coals dance around the perimeter of the only five spaces where his Aircraft Carrier can possibly be. I waste guesses. I guess some spaces twice, although Dad doesn't seem to notice. But what I'm most occupied with is telepathic bulletins. As his guesses get quieter, more discouraged, and further apart, I stare down at the dinky little Destroyer stationed on D9 and 10 and I chant to myself, *D9, D9.*

And Dad looks up and says, "C7?"

Earlier we played Thousand Rummy. And just as on the previous days, Dad was the one to draw the ace of spades. If it was Gin, Thousand Rummy, or even Concentration, Dad would sit there in his pajamas (he sometimes wears his pajamas all day now), press his lips together decisively, and flip over a card . . . and there it would be.

The ace of spades, the Death Card.

How can this keep happening? It's getting so that we wait for the ace of spades. It seems to look for Dad. Since we stopped seeing Fritz and ended the medicines, a sense of doom sits over Dad like a mist.

So there it is, Dad seems to say. He looks at the card like he's been expecting it. He drops his head into his hands like a condemned man. The writing on the card, which seemed innocent before he got sick, seems to have turned into an ominous message.

DEBONNAIRE, OLEET PLAYING CARD CO.,
MOUNT VERNON, N.Y. "SUPERKOTED"™

What does this mean to Dad?

The ace of spades stands on its unipod and stares my father down. It's a heart upside down. It's the opposite of a heart.

POUNDS OF CURE

Mom and I return to the house after a Saturday afternoon in the library.

"Whatcha got there?" Marty asks. Dad trails him into the dining room.

Each of us dumps a double armload of reading material on the table. I have nine books, including *Affirmations in the Key of Health* by Lillian Drakava; *Make Up Your Mind: Self-Empowerment Through Mood Selection* by R. Candelbaum, MD; *Go for the Joy* by Sybil Lucien-Simple, MSW; and a thinner one called *Darkness Manifest* by an award-winning novelist, as well as a stack of journal and magazine articles, some photocopied and some printed off the computer.

On the way there, Mom said she was lucky, in this difficult time, to have a teenage son with my capacity for understanding human nature. I have to admit that it was strangely fun finding books that described what Dad was going through. There were almost too many matches to choose. When I asked the librarian how I could tell if a book was any good, he told me to look for letters after the person's name. A shelf full of credentials—PhD, EdD, LICSW, and DDiv—cleared its throat at me, but I chose some authors with no letters, like the novelist (ultrasad eyes, extra neck skin), just because I liked their pictures.

"You can tell a lot from their pictures," Linda agrees, picking up books and flipping them over.

The books in Mom's stack include *Feed Your Brain* by Wilbert and Orralie Curtis, *The Feel Good Vitamin Bible* from the publishers of *Feel Good* magazine, and *Peace Without Pills: How Eating Right Can Replace Costly and Potentially Harmful Psychotropic Medications* by Evgenia Sutter, CNC. Behind the crinkly, scuffed plastic library covers, the smiling Curtises wear matching red-and-white checked shirts and hold out palmfuls of unprocessed grain. Evgenia Sutter has long brown hair and wears a white lab jacket with eyeglasses in the pocket.

Some faces are like a hard pill. Others are more of a loose powder. One of them will be the cure for what ails Dad.

AUTODIDACT

Mom stays up late cramming information from her library books and articles. She reads paragraphs aloud, as if putting words in the air will pollinate Dad with a cure.

Like most Americans, she says, she has always known the basics about proper nutrition without bothering to follow them. But now, like the cop or soldier in the movies whose buddy is killed, she announces, "This time, it's personal." She memorizes the foods and supplements that provide B vitamins 1 (thiamine), 2 (riboflavin), 3 (niacin), 6 (pyridoxine), and 12 (cyanocobalamin), as well as folic acid, inositol, vitamins C and E; crucial minerals such as calcium, chromium, magnesium, selenium, iron, iodine, and zinc; and the amino acids gamma-aminobutyric acid (GABA), S-adenosyl L-methionine (SAMe), serotonin, melatonin, L-tryptophan, 5-hydroxytryptophan (5-HTP), DL-phenylalanine (DLPA), trimethylglycine (TMG), omega-3 fatty acids, and tyrosine.

These substances, Mom learns, improve brain function, restoring the moistness and flexibility of certain membranes and helping brain cells to manufacture the chemicals they need to keep the neurotransmitters signaling. But so many expert opinions, she tells us, are difficult to sort out. One book says that serotonin and melatonin are chemicals that the brain will produce after a body consumes the right combination of foods. In another book, melatonin and seratonin are capsules you can buy in the health food store. If both are true, where did the chemicals for the capsules come from? Mom shudders. Maybe she's getting morbid because it's so late (Dad is already in bed and listening to a talk show on the radio), but as I pass by her chair, she tells me her thoughts are taking a ghoulish turn. You hear about gravediggers and organ thieves. Is someone stealing brains and selling the chemicals from them?

The experts in Mom's books agree that someone with Dad's symptoms should avoid coffee and cola, alcohol, sugar, and dairy products. But a major source of two crucial substances, calcium (helps to maintain a healthy central nervous system) and tyrosine (stimulates the brain's production of norepinephrine), is cheese. Mom wonders aloud if she should give him cheese or not. Should she look for a special, nondairy cheese? Kosher cheese? And where would she find extract of *Griffonia simplicifolia*, an African plant (and source of 5-hydroxytryptophan)?

And, Mom wants to know, what about Evgenia Sutter's habit of saying "widely celebrated in Europe," "available inexpensively in Europe," and "exhaustively tested throughout Europe"? Have these chemicals been tested in America? Are they known by the same names here? Do they maybe have a "street name"?

Mom tells me she fell asleep earlier this evening and had a nightmare that she was arrested for trying to procure *Griffonia simplicifolia* in a back alley. She describes the dream: A bus ride back to New York, the city she thought she had left for good. Returning just once more, for Dad's sake. Walking late at night from playground to decrepit coffee shop to back alley. Looking over her shoulder whenever she hears a sound. She can't find the right address, the city makes no sense. The layout of the city resembles Granada, Spain. Has New York really changed so much since she left? When she finds the place where the deal will go down, it's an alley behind a deserted high-rise. A gaunt, shivering figure approaches and asks for the password.

"Ignorance."

"No."

"Impotence."

"No."

"Hegemony?"

"No."

"Fluoridization?"

"Okay."

"How much?" she asks.

"Two thousand," he says. "Cash." Mom has only twelve dollars. In the dream, she forgets that she can go to an ATM. She finds a knife in her pocket, Grandpa Eddie's old fishing knife. The knife flashes under the streetlight, and a siren begins to wail.

Hours later Mom's reading lamp is still on.

"Mom, go to bed. It's the middle of the night. You're asleep again."

"I never meant to cause any harm," she says out loud.

"It all seemed so simple," she says.

"Mom, you need to stop reading."

I shake her awake. The tip of her index finger is white where she has used it as a bookmark.

LIGHT

The four of us are playing Monopoly in the dining room when Uncle Marty struggles into the house with his arms around a box, walking it in on top of one shoe.

"Good grief," says Mom. Mom, Linda, and Dad crowd around him while I stabilize the game. Mom was winning.

"You thought Christmas was over," he tells the family, "but it's not. A late Christmas gift for the lord of the manor—my big brother, Bill."

Even Dad is impressed. When Marty lays the mammoth gift in the center of the living room, Dad crouches over it to peel away the Christmas paper. Large block letters on the side of the box say VITA-LITE.

"I can't get the flaps open," Dad says over his shoulder.

"I've got it, bro, no problem." Marty borrows my pocket knife and pries off the heavy-duty staples.

Dad removes several sheets of crumpled newsprint and slides out the light box. It's about the size and depth of a small kitchen table. Marty pulls out the rear leg to stand it upright.

"Thank you, Marty," Dad says.

"Don't thank me yet. Wait till you see this."

Marty crawls under the Christmas tree, reaches for the outlet, and unplugs the holiday lights.

"Oh, no!" Mom complains.

"Mom," Linda says, "it's January eighteenth. It had to happen sooner or later."

"But it was so cheerful." She drops into a seat in the conversation area.

"Sorry, Adele," Marty says. "But this thing uses a good flow of juice. I wouldn't want you to short anything out."

Half the lights in the house pulse, then flicker. The part of the living room where Dad is gets flooded with white light, like a prison courtyard during an attempted break.

"Aack," Linda says, lifting an arm to shield her face.

"I think it's too strong," Mom agrees.

"But this could be just the thing for Bill," Marty argues. "Don't close your eyes, bro—open them. You have to have them open so it can act on your retinas."

"It's going to blind him."

"No, it has to be strong in order to work. Look at him—I think he looks better already!"

"That's because he's getting a tan," says Linda.

"Such a costly gift, Marty," Mom says. "You must have spent several hundred dollars." Normally Dad would have said something like this too. He was always warning Marty that his credit card balances were too high.

"It's just a way of saying thank you, Bill, for all the support you've given me this year, with everything I've gone through. I can honestly say that this has been the worst year of my life. Without you to talk to, I don't think I would have made it." He presses one eye with the back of his knuckles.

Then he takes Dad by the elbow. "Sit down, bro, and I'll tell you more about how it works. This unit runs at twenty thousand lux—that's up to forty times the brightness of normal indoor light!"

"What good does that do?" Linda asks.

"You just sit in front of the light each morning—"

"For how long?" Mom asks.

"Up to about an hour—and the light travels up your optic nerve and basically tricks your brain into thinking it's summer. The light tinkers with the chemicals in your brain, and you, you know, just stop being depressed. Everyone is happier in the summer and sadder in the winter. Haven't you ever felt that way? Doesn't it make sense?"

"The theory sounds plausible," Mom says. "But the execution is so *extreme*."

"It only seems that way, Adele. You find yourself getting used to it. Come on, bro, we'll sit in front of it together and test it out. You don't have to look right into it, you just glance at it from time to time. The instructions say you can read if you want to, or knit. Come on, buddy."

"Dad knits?" Linda asks.

"It's so big—," Marty begins.

"I hadn't noticed," Mom says.

"It's so big that I suggest you decide on a permanent spot for it," Marty continues. "So it won't be in the way."

"Why don't you put it against the north wall there," I tell him, referring to the divider between the living room and the kitchen. "That way Dad can get light from this in the early morning, and then natural sunlight from the picture window in the afternoon."

"Marty," says Mom, "all kidding aside, I just have to question whether this is really safe."

Marty drops into the loveseat opposite Mom. "I thought you'd all be pleased, Adele. This technique is medically approved. By the American Medical Association and the National Institutes of Mental Health."

"And the electrical utilities, no doubt," Mom says. "I'm sorry, Marty. I shouldn't joke. I do appreciate that you're only trying to help."

At last I join the family in the living room. "Well, I think it makes a lot of sense," I say, as if I just decided.

"Good boy," Marty says, and winks at me.

The others have no idea that this was all my suggestion. I read about it, I researched it on the Internet before Christmas, and I got Marty to pay $729 for it. Soon, I know, Dad will be well, and the expense will have been worth it.

"It's so *bright*, though, Billy," Mom says. "Just look at it. I'd be afraid of it burning a hole in my retina or something. Marty, isn't it dangerous to look directly into the sun?"

"Mom, this isn't anything like the sun. The sun is—I don't know—probably a million lux, probably. A lot more than this, anyway. And remember: It's only for a few weeks."

"Well," Mom says, "I speak on behalf of my husband when I say that it's very impressive, dangerous or not." Mom all at once looks younger—but just a couple of months younger, like the way she looked when we started going to Fritz.

"Why don't we try an experiment?" Marty suggests.

"Everyone, make note of your mood right now. Then we'll try it for ten minutes and see if anyone feels better."

"Okay," Linda says, "name your mood. Amused. Next?"

"I didn't mean name your mood like name that tune, hon. I just meant make a mental note of it to yourself."

Mom, Dad, and Marty line up on the couch facing the north wall, while Linda and I sit on the floor in front of them.

Actually, once I experience the light I almost think Mom has a point. Its intensity is hard to get used to, like it might burn away even the memory of color. But Dad seems calm. So we keep doing it.

TREATMENT REPORT: DAY 60

The books contain so many valuable suggestions that it's hard to know what to choose. But after deliberating, I choose three areas: affirmations, occupational rehabilitation, and light therapy. Mom feels that diet and exercise are surefire winners. Linda wants to work on aromatherapy.

So Mom presents a plan for the three of us, the treatment team. Already, Linda has begun wafting Kleenexes saturated with lemon oil under Dad's nose. Every time she does this, his eyebrows shoot up. The lemon oil has a piercingly clean smell, like furniture cleaner or dishwashing liquid. Mom has determined a nutritional baseline for Dad. Each day he will eat a bowl of hot bran cereal, an ounce of aged natural cheese, a slice of health bread with natural peanut butter, a serving of seafood, a cooked salad of kale and onions, a mound of navy beans sprinkled with brewer's yeast, and twenty pomegranate seeds. The Curtises call these the Seven Brain Foods. Mom likes the idea of brain foods, because in addition to making Dad less happy and less confident, the depression has also made him less smart.

As for the remaining approaches, first thing in the morning Dad will be expected to switch on his light box and sit in front of it while Mom reads him the most uplifting highlights from the morning newspaper. When I take over after school, I'll work with Dad for fifteen minutes on repeating powerful phrases: "I am well." "I am happy." "The universe is moving toward perfection." Afterward, we'll spend an hour or two on cards, board games, and educational television—as long as Dad can stay still. No junk TV, like reality shows or cop shows—only things that are soothing and that elevate the mind. After Mom gets home and we have dinner, Mom will lead him through a program of calisthenics demanding enough to tire him out but not so stimulating that they would wake him up at night. I'll keep periodic records showing changes in sleep, appetite, concentration, and mood.

A MULTIPRONGED PLAN

"I call that a plan," Linda says.

"Okay, but . . ."

"You have an objection?" Mom asks.

Although I hate to be a wellness wet blanket, I have to ask how, if we try so many different treatments at once, we will be able to tell which ones are working.

"What about the whole idea of the scientific method? Controls and variables. You maintain the same conditions for a set period of time and change just one factor."

"You don't have to tell me about the scientific method," Mom says. She seems miffed that I haven't swooned over her program.

"Well, what if one of these treatments works and the others don't? How will we know to keep doing the right thing? Or what if one of them causes him to backslide, and they cancel each other out?"

"Well." Mom places her glasses on top of her head. "I

appreciate what you're saying, Billy, but I think, given the fact that your father has already been ill for a couple of months, we should try everything we can in order to save time, even if that means employing many treatments at once and not developing the kind of complete data set you think would be so edifying."

"I totally agree with Mom," Linda adds. "You're going off on a tangent as usual. Don't you even care whether Dad gets back to normal?"

"Of course I do. Don't you care about anything other than agreeing with Mom? Mom, say Dad suddenly starts to get better—"

"Then he gets better, right? And that's what we want. End of story."

TREATMENT REPORT: DAY 61

The treatment team has rolled out Dad's complete new wellness program, and we are off to an excellent start. We started slow on the light box (phototherapy), with just twenty minutes, per orders of Mom, who is still skeptical. Then did twenty of each affirmation. Dad ate at least a bit of all his brain foods, plus two handfuls of nuts. When Mom came home he moved gamely through his calisthenics. Linda did two sessions of wafts.

TREATMENT REPORT: DAY 62

Today Dad had trouble focusing on Monopoly and staying in his chair. I had to explain his old strategy back to him, of buying every possible property even if it meant mortgaging something until he passed Go. Discouraging. But Linda came home with nachos and Dad wanted some, even though junk food is against the program. Mom said it was good that he had an appetite, so he ate a few pieces, but from now on when Linda and I are at home we will have to eat what Dad's eating. We agree that calisthenics are helping him sleep. He is learning the affirmations well and could probably do them alone.

A NIGHT OUT: PART I

On Thursday afternoon the phone rings. Linda is making bead jewelry in her room with her little friend Jodie. Dad is trying to nap on the couch, so after the first ring I answer the phone in my parents' bedroom instead of the kitchen.

"You'd better sit down," Gordon says.

"Why?"

"Are you sitting down?"

"Yes." I sit on the edge of my parents' bed.

"I have tickets to Buddy Guy tomorrow night. In Boston."

"What?"

"Buddy Guy. At Berklee College. My dad got the tickets as a surprise, and we were going to go together, but he has a business thing and he can't go. It's a miracle, Bilbo—Buddy Guy. My dad said we could take the train in *by ourselves*. The concert starts at eight fifteen. We pick you up at seven o'clock. He gave us money to go out to eat afterward—"

"Whoa. I just have to make sure I can go."

"Whoa back. You would consider missing a Buddy Guy concert? It's free. We have great seats. You don't have to pay a cent."

"I know. But sometimes I have to babysit," I whisper.

"For your sister?"

"No, for, you know, my dad. I didn't mean to say babysit. I meant to say watch, or just sit with. My mother works, and my sister is too young. You know, he's sick. He doesn't stay home by himself."

"That's right." In the silence that follows looms the thing I haven't been mentioning. Gordy is here again, in our living room, while Dad walks back and forth without talking to him. How could he understand this? I barely understand it myself.

"I'm sorry," Gordy continues. "I shouldn't put the pressure on. It's just—"

"Just what?"

"Well, when my mom was really sick, my dad hired a nurse. Two nurses actually. Around the clock. He had to work a lot, that's why. But I get it, I completely understand. So . . ."

Suddenly going to a concert by Buddy Guy, legendary

Chicago bluesman, is what I want more than anything in the world. Sitting on a commuter train that's nearly empty because everyone's going in the opposite direction. We each have our own bench, so we talk to one another across the aisle. Gordy drums the metal part of the seat in front of him while we hum "Ninety-Nine and One Half" and "What Kind of Woman Is This?" We eat Chinese food or pizza in a restaurant where the customers are all city kids. Just us, in the city at night. No adults telling us what to do.

"How would we get home, anyway?"

"We take the train home, too. My dad's going to pick us up at the station. We have it all worked out, Bilbo. The whole situation is ready, it's just waiting for you to step into it. I could ask somebody else, but I thought you were the one who would really appreciate it. Anyway . . ."

"I think I can. I'll ask. Assume that I'll go, okay? Assume that I'm going, unless you hear otherwise. No, wait—I really have to think about this."

"If you can't go, I'll see if Mitchell wants to. Or Andy. Are you a definite yes? Do you want to give me their phone numbers just in case? Or should I wait to hear back from you first?"

"No, I'm almost definitely a yes. Assume I'll go."

"That was confusing. But I completely understand."

"I have to go," I whisper. My voice got loud there for a minute when I pictured tomorrow night in Boston. It was almost like I was there, even.

When I hang up the phone and walk down the hall, Dad is waiting on the living-room couch.

"Is something wrong, Billy? Did someone get hurt?"

"No, no one is hurt."

"From the tone of your voice, I thought something was wrong."

"It's okay, Dad. It was just Gordon."

"Should we watch TV, then?"

"Yes. Let's watch TV."

A NIGHT OUT: PART 2

When Mom gets home from work, she brushes the snow off her coat and drops a pile of museum papers and American history journals on the coffee table.

"God, I hate dealing with the public. You wouldn't believe how many of these local types think just because you're a museum you want to hear about every generation of the family that ever touched a piece of leather. And the pictures. And the diaries. And the letters. And would we *pay* for the letters."

"I thought you liked all that stuff, Mom."

"I couldn't get them to leave!"

I follow her around until she seems settled. I've decided to use the announcement method.

"I'm going out tomorrow night."

"Where are you going?"

"Gordy has tickets for a concert."

"Who's playing?"

"Buddy Guy."

"Ah, Buddy Guy! Bill?"

"Yes?" My father appears in the hall, already wearing pajamas.

"Billy's going to a Buddy Guy concert."

"Okay. . . . Enjoy yourself."

"It's not till tomorrow, Dad."

Dad doesn't seem too interested. Ordinarily, he would try to impersonate an old bluesman, the way John Belushi did.

"The tickets are free. We're going to take the train into Boston and go out to eat afterward."

"Sounds like a great time." Mom opens the dishwasher and stacks some clean plates.

"Let me do that, Mom."

I've never gone to Boston by myself, but it seems that, rather than our bad situation causing Mom to clamp down on me more than normal, it's distracted her enough that she doesn't question what I'm doing. This is an unexpected side benefit, a victory. I'm about to go into Boston at night, alone, with Gordy.

More and more, the concert sounds like a great opportunity. Right before Mom's arrival, while watching TV with Dad, I imagined eating in some hole-in-the-wall near the auditorium and seeing a couple of Buddy Guy's musicians come in for a drink or a late supper after the show. They'd be wearing sharp suits with the necktie undone and possibly carrying an instrument case. Although that might be ridiculous, now that I think of it—they must have roadies to carry the instruments. "Bravo!" Gordy and I might shout as they walked in the door. We'd jump to our feet for a standing ovation that would make the rest of the diners stare. *You boys like the old music?* one would ask, throwing a bill to the bartender and bringing his scotch to our table. Although Gordy would hold up most of our end, the musicians would be incredulous meeting two kids who could talk to them about their work. When it was time for our train to leave, the musicians would clasp us on the shoulder and we'd all agree to keep in touch. *Best of luck, kids. Don't ever change.*

"Okay, they're picking me up at seven."

"That's not going to work."

"What?"

"I have to stay a little late tomorrow. A group of researchers are coming all the way from Pennsylvania to spend the day in our archives, and I have to keep the library open for them."

"Can't Pudge do it?"

"Pudge. Pudge has some kind of fund-raiser he has to go to. You know, like a dress-up thing. He's not going to stay late at the Brooksbie."

"What about Mrs. Arabian? She's a volunteer. Won't she do whatever you tell her to?"

"Billy, I don't want to push it. I've already asked for enough special treatment. I just want to do the Pennsylvanian thing and make myself useful."

"Could you even ask Mrs. Arabian?"

"Billy. Do you have any idea how many people in the entire United States have a job that allows them to work from two thirty to six? Me. Just me. I'm the only one."

"So I have to stay home while you're at work?"

"That's what I expect. If I came home and found you gone, I'd be upset."

"What about Linda?" I ask.

"What about her?"

"She can't watch Dad?"

"Come on, Billy. You know she's too young."

"You won't ask Mrs. Arabian?"

"Will you stop it, please? You're getting on my nerves."

"I'll have to call Gordy, then. I'll have to tell him I can't go."

Now Gordy will ride the train with Mitchell, or worse, Andy, who would make inappropriate comments, act immature, and call his parents every half hour to let them know he was okay. It would all be wasted on him.

"I have an idea," Mom says. She's poking the pot of navy beans that were soaked all day, to see whether they're tender enough. "How about getting Marty to cover for you?"

"Marty?"

"Why not? He could come over and sit with Dad between when you leave and when I get home."

"That's a great idea."

"But I don't want you going anywhere until Marty arrives. Got that?"

"Sure."

"Hey. Got that?"

"Yep."

A NIGHT OUT: PART 3

I call Marty from the bedroom so I won't be in Mom's way in the kitchen. His cell phone rings five times.

"Bro?"

"Marty, it's Billy."

"Who is it? Sorry, it's noisy here."

"It's Billy, Marty."

"Billy! Good to hear from you. Is everything okay at home?"

"Yeah, it's fine. I need to ask for your help. Could you come and sit with Dad for an hour tomorrow night?"

"Sure! I'd love to. No problem."

"Thanks. Mom's working late and I need to leave to go to a concert. Buddy Guy. In Boston."

"That's great, Billy, just great. Now, what time would you want me there?"

"By seven o'clock."

"Seven o'clock. Just a minute. Hold on and I'll be right back to you."

Marty is part owner of a bar and restaurant in the next town. I hear him ask a question of someone else in the bar, probably his partner. The sounds of the business—clinking glasses, a cash register drawer, a cart full of dishes—unpause my mental movie about tomorrow night. The musicians are leaving. They clasp us on the shoulder, shake our hands. *Best of luck, kids. Keep in touch. And if you ever need a favor . . .*

"You're in luck. I can be there by seven thirty," Marty is saying.

"Seven thirty, not seven?"

"Seven thirty. Best I can do. Although I'm glad to do it. I want to talk to Bill anyway. I have some investment ideas I'd like to run by him."

"Seven thirty won't work. Is there any way you could be here earlier?"

"No, I can't. I wish I could, though."

Now Andy will sit with Gordy in the restaurant. The musicians will come by with their glasses of scotch and start talking to Andy, not to me. Andy will get to stand outside with them while they smoke. Andy will insult them by letting his eyes drift over the shoulder of Orlando Wright, Buddy's bass player, to the TV over the bar, and becoming rapt in a game show on which a supermodel is being forced to eat a bucket of slugs.

"I can't go to the concert, then."

"Gee, I'm sorry. I really wish I could help you out, Billy. I'm awful sorry."

"Thanks, anyway. I know how it must be, having your own business. You always have to be there, right?"

"That's right. Look, is there anybody else you could ask?"

"Not really. There are people. But nobody who really knows how to take care of Dad."

"Well, Billy, if things change and seven thirty would work out, will you call me right back?"

"I will. I'll call you right back."

A NIGHT OUT: PART 4

My only chance now is to find a way of getting there without taking the train. Someone will have to drive us all the
way to Boston, all the way to Berklee Performance Center.
It can't be Gordy's father, he already has something to do.
It can't be Mom—she'll be at work. It can't be Marty—he'll
be here. It can't be Dad, either. Whoever it is, we would
have to leave the house at exactly seven thirty, no later. The
driver will speed. We will fly down Route 1 to the auditorium, assuming there is no traffic. We will not look for
parking spaces. We will be ejected, thrown, rolled, whatever, out of the car right at the entrance, and the driver will
take off. We will run, panting, into the building with our
tickets out, past the ushers, into a darkened auditorium,
the last people to take their seats, provided the show hasn't
already started, in which case we might be asked to wait,
during the opening number, right inside the door. Who can
I find? Who will help me?

What, you kids are planning on taking the train? Nobody should take a train on a night like this. Here, take the limo.

Who can I find?

I can't find anyone.

A NIGHT OUT: PART 5

Okay. I can do this. I can call Gordy and tell him I can't make it to the concert tomorrow. He can invite someone else. I can call Gordy and tell him to take Mitchell or Andy, although Andy will laugh at the wrong times. Andy will also sing along loudly with any song he's heard before, drowning out Buddy Guy's one-time interpretation, unrecorded and unique to this Berklee College concert, ruining it for those immediately around him.

I can do this. I'm lifting the phone. I'm dialing.

A NIGHT OUT: PART 6

It's funny what's happening right now. I had meant to call Gordy yesterday and tell him I couldn't go. I dialed and everything with the best of intentions. But instead I called Marty and told him to come at seven thirty. It's not that I feel angry or rebellious or anything. I'm just sort of watching myself from the outside—watching myself settle Dad in front of the TV and tell him to sit tight for a few minutes until Marty arrives, watching the car pull up, and watching myself go.

I go.

GOING

On the train, knowing I'm where I shouldn't be sharpens my senses. The world is shouting at me: SCHRAFFT'S in pink neon from a clock tower like a cathedral, H. P. HOOD on the big dairy office building. The graffiti on the empty freight cars are strangers shouting "I was here." On the Boston Sand and Gravel plant, a big sign cautions ACCIDENTS HAVE NO HOLIDAYS.

With no cell phone, I can't get pulled back. No one knows my location for sure, though they could hazard a guess. Watching father-son dyads board in matching Bruins jackets, I try not to think about Dad alone. Looking to the right as the train crosses the Charles River, I try not to think about Dad's dream of sinking in the metal box. When we see the suspension bridge topped with two Washington Monuments and lit in blue lights, the father-son dyads are already standing, so we elbow around them, through the station, and between the ticket scalpers outside. This is Boston. Streetlamps shining through maple trees with polluted-looking branches. Double-parked cars, brick buildings with garbage bags growing like mushrooms at the foot.

We take the Green Line to the Hynes/ICA stop. Crossing Boylston, we do a curb dance as an unmarked car and two cruisers careen around the corner, sirens barking. Drunks ask us croakily for a cigarette, and a woman asks for money to buy formula for her grandbaby. See? None of this would be happening in Hawthorne.

The theater is big, a thousand seats, though not anywhere near as big as the arena at North Station. It feels right to be here instead of home. The theater is already dark and Buddy's band is already performing when we scuttle to our seats in the front row.

THOUGHTS THAT INTRUDE
ON MY ENJOYMENT,
ALTHOUGH THEY DON'T ACTUALLY
RUIN THE CONCERT FOR ME

a. This should be fun.

b. This is going to be fun.

c. This should really be a lot of fun.

d. Obviously, there's been a serious lack of music in my life lately. Unless you count the school assembly that featured a performance by the Hawtones, our high school a cappella group. They are known in a cappella circles for their unique medley of classic songs about New England ("Massachusetts," "Old Cape Cod," "Charlie on the MTA"). I'm sure it plays better on the road than it does back home in Hawthorne, in the heart of the region they are singing about.

e. I met someone my age once who had a subscription to the Boston Symphony Orchestra and sat in the same seat every year, at the edge of the right balcony, overhanging the musicians. He impressed me as quite the egghead until he said the main reason he liked going was to feel the vibrations against his skin. That's something you miss when you listen to music on headphones.

f. Gordy just gave me the quick-glance-nod-and-smile-with-eyebrows-raised. He's obviously having fun. Good for him.

g. I wonder what we're going to eat later.

h. For a while Dad was getting me to sing his favorite tenor/baritone opera duets with him, with the volume of the CD turned way up. Especially a duet from *The Pearl Fishers*, in which a pair of best friends are in love with the same woman. "It's her! It's that goddess!" he would sing in French. "She threads her way through the crowd." And if Mom walked into the room at that moment, he would really play it up. Toward the conclusion of the song, some falsely tense music signals the strife in the friends' relationship. It always reminded me of the soundtrack to an action movie with planes colliding or planets exploding. It's like someone went in with a Roto-Rooter and churned up the orchestra, and you could tell the story would come to a bad end. But the two friends sing, "Nothing must separate us! Let's pledge to always remain friends!" Slashes from the strings, and a big crescendo: "Let's stay united UNTI-I-I-IL death!" And the orchestra does a bunch of big chords, like the words THE END rolling across a movie screen not once but four times.

He asked me to sing that with him a few weeks before the Gordy incident, but I was just leaving for Mitchell's to watch a movie. I see now that that happened right when Dad was first getting sick. Maybe I wish I had gone along with it?

i. Now Buddy Guy has stepped off the stage and is traveling up the aisle with his guitar. (One of the sound men follows him with an extension cord coiled around his shoulder.) I don't think the restaurant-networking thing is going to happen, but I do think he just nodded at me.

TREATMENT REPORT: DAY 66

Although there was no one to see what was happening during the half hour that Dad was left alone, it seems to have been pretty bad. Dad didn't know what had happened to me, he invented all kinds of things in his mind, and he ended up calling the police. Marty sent the police away as soon as he got here.

"I didn't want to rat you out to your mother, Billy," he told me in the kitchen when I got home. "Believe me, it totally killed me, and I completely remember what it was like to be a kid. But I was so concerned for your dad that I had to say something. You forgive me, don't you, buddy?"

Mom had stayed at the Brooksbie until ten thirty with the Pennsylvanians, so she had only been home for an hour when I got back. Marty had everything under control by then. After Marty spoke to me Mom took me to the utility room, where Dad, Marty, and even Linda couldn't see or hear us.

"We worked so hard to set up a complete, elaborate, minute-by-minute plan for caring for your father," she said, "and you have selfishly bungled it.

"Did you see how your father looked tonight?" she continued, whispering. "How white and shaky? What do you think he looked like at seven thirty when Marty got here? He doesn't even know if he can trust us anymore. He doesn't even know if at any minute he'll be left by himself to do who knows what."

Mom was so upset that she didn't even say the one thing I was counting on: "I hope you enjoyed yourself," after which I had planned to say, "I sure did!" Then I would tell her that I really had wanted to go to the concert and I didn't think she had lifted a finger to make it happen. But instead I started saying, "I'm sorry. I'm sorry. I'll make it up to you. I promise." Something about Dad looking so white and weird, and the house being so quiet when I came in, and all four of them looking at me with an accusation (except Dad, really, because he doesn't have that much expression).

Around midnight Mom came to my room. I was lying there watching my Escher drawing shift in a square of street light, foreground, background, foreground, background, anything but solid ground. Mom said she understood a little bit of what I was going through, and maybe she should have tried harder to let me go to the concert. Then she said that in fairness to me, Linda was going to have to come home right after school too.

And that was today's change to the treatment plan.

AN AERIAL VIEW OF MOM AND DAD

Some nights my mind is a night watchman. It leaves my body and roams the house checking on everyone. My mental bedroom slippers are becoming as worn as the carpet Dad makes his circuit on. I don't think this is a bad thing. If I can be sure everyone is sleeping, then I can sleep too.

Here is the front door with both a doorbell and a knocker. Here are some shoes and boots, once wet or sandy, on a hard plastic mat inside the door. Here is the plate-glass window with floor-length draperies. Here is the conversation area, littered with schoolbooks, Brooksbie papers, and old *Newsweek*s. Here are throw pillows with sayings on them: "I Don't Do Perky," "Welcome to Our Piece of Paradise," "Mothers Nurture the Flowers in the Garden of Life," "Your Point Is?" One pillow has fallen under the big square coffee table. I'll pull it out and put it on the couch. There.

I mustn't trip over the boxes on the floor. Fragile items

are contained in them. Linda got exasperated and started taking the decorations off the Christmas tree. I know what I'll do. I won't walk anymore. I'll float.

Here is the dining room. The curtains are open and the backyard is dark. Bars of light appear between the slats of the back fence when a car passes on the highway, like the moving pattern on the top of a jukebox. Here is the kitchen. An oil painting of a chicken, done by one of Mom's friends at Brooksbie, looks friendly in the daytime but evil now. Its hard chicken eyes are the brightest spot in the room. They're the kind of eyes that follow you. Bad chicken! Why does it have to look so real?

I float along the hallway with its wall-to-wall carpet. It was a good idea, putting carpet here, so if you were walking, and someone else were sleeping, you wouldn't wake them up. Linda's room. Linda is sleeping, of course. She sleeps under a Garfield comforter, holding a plush Garfield, and beneath a photo collage of all the mad times she's had with her shadow, Jodie. Garfield is her night watchman.

The big bathroom has a shower curtain with a graphic design of black-and-white blocks. No one has cleaned the tub for a while. Who can be bothered? Someone should step up for that. Not me. People always end up doing the things that are most important. If it were important, someone would surely do it. Ergo, it is not important. Here is the laundry hamper. It's full. We've gotten accustomed to seeing one another in a lot of the same clothes over and over again. I don't even remember what I have in there. It will be exciting to find out, when that day comes. It will be like getting new clothes.

Now I'm at the door to my parents' room. The door is open a bit, not latched. I won't make a sound. Should I go in, or leave them to their privacy? I'll go in, just to check. I push against the door with all the purchase I can get in my floating state. My back rubs against the ceiling. There is their bed, with piles of clothes on the floor on either side. There is their bathroom, the sink piled up with laxatives and other things I don't want to know about. And there they are: two parents, joined at the hand.

Their hands meet with the palms crossed, the elbows bent, so the two arms form one W. Mom's arm is bare—she's wearing a sleeveless nightgown. Dad's arm is in a pajama sleeve with a frayed cuff. Their faces are sixteen inches apart.

Dad's age has seemed to change while he's been sick. Sometimes he seems old. Other times he seems young.

Right now he's young, listening to Mom. (It's so serious in here!) His profile doesn't look adult. His nose is short, and his upper lip rises in an expectant way. He reminds me of someone, but I don't know who. A light from the bedside table on the right, an old porcelain one of Grandma's with a rose painted on it, is reflected in Dad's forehead. Now I know who it is—*me*. He looks just like me when I had my silhouette done out of black paper when I was ten. When did he start to look like me, instead of me looking like him?

On the left is a clock radio. When each minute goes by, two flaps that make up the numerals break apart and recombine to make up a new number. Right now it says 12:21. Between 12:21 and 12:22, eight cars go by on the highway behind the house.

Mom and Dad stare into one another's eyes. Three times the minute changes. Twenty-six cars go by on the highway. Mom's lips move. At first, her having spoken is so unexpected that it's difficult to realize what she's said: "Magnolia."

Dad moistens his lips. He swallows, and his forehead tightens for a second, which makes the shiny spot jump almost to his hairline, then back down again. A car door slams in a driveway a few houses down the hill. The lamp goes "tink" for no reason, in that way electrical appliances sometimes do.

"Marigold." Where did that come from? From Dad. His lips are still moving. He squeezes Mom's hand, like a twitch, and then relaxes. He swallows again.

Mom stares. It seems to be a new stare, more forceful, lower and more insistent, even though she hasn't moved. Maybe the depth and hypnotic quality of her eyes changed.

"Narcissus," Mom has said. Mom's voice is a city voice. She's having him name a flower for every letter of the alphabet. I didn't know they played this game. I didn't know Mom had games of her own, apart from the ones I play with Dad. I thought I knew everything about these people.

The numbers on the clock turn over again. Why hasn't Dad answered? Nasturtium would be a good answer. A pattern of lilies, in the sheets, surrounds their heads. Lines of dust gather in the creases of the folding closet door. I would definitely go with nasturtium.

A motorcycle spits by on the highway, and the corners of Dad's mouth jump. He can't help it. The clock says 12:32. Mom stares.

Why hasn't he said nasturtium? I want to get between them and shake things up.

"Narcissus," he says.

Mom doesn't take her eyes from his. A tendon stands out on the side of her wrist.

"I already said narcissus," she says.

Dad moistens his lips again. "Okay," he says. He waits. Mom waits. Oh, no. I think I fell asleep for a fractosecond. I am literally falling down on the job here. Which one had Mom said, nasturtium or narcissus? Well, whichever one it was, why doesn't Dad say the other one?

Mom's hand slowly releases its grip on Dad's. Their hands make a sucking sound as they pull apart.

Mom rolls over. She's facing the ceiling. She's facing *me*. She closes her eyes, hiding the tiredness that Dad isn't meant to see.

I'm falling again. It's 12:47. For this minute at least, everyone in the house is asleep.

TREATMENT REPORT: DAY 68

Occupational therapy keeps both Dad and me busy after school, but I can't help feeling discouraged. When we watch *Painting with the Light-Teacher* at four p.m., Dad keeps saying, "How does he do that?" I selected the show because it is wholesome, educational, nonviolent, etc., but it is *way* below Dad's level as an artist. In fact, he always laughed at the show before, calling the Light-Teacher a gimmicky charlatan.

I see now that by taking my trip to Boston, I shot myself in the foot. Because now that Linda has to stay home out of fairness to me, Jodie is always here, the three of us plus Dad, and I am in charge of the household, the prisoner of my night of freedom.

BARRETTE

"I'm tired of the food you serve here, Billy," Jodie says. She is helping Linda pick the seeds out of a pomegranate.

"We don't 'serve' anything here. This isn't a restaurant."

"Do you like pizza, Mr. Morrison?" she calls into the next room.

"Yes."

"Why don't you get him a pizza?"

"Because he can't eat pizza right now, and he isn't hungry, anyway."

"Well, all right," Dad says.

"Dad, since when have you felt hungry? Jodie, didn't Linda tell you he's on a restricted diet?"

"Why?" Jodie asks. "He already looks awfully skinny to me."

"I can't explain the whole thing to you. It's very complex, and it involves enzymes and things like that. My mother can tell you."

"It's almost time for your wafts, Dad," Linda says. She puts the bowl containing the pomegranate and its seeds aside. She takes a lemon half out of the refrigerator and peels off the plastic wrap.

"What's a waft?" Jodie asks.

"It's a special technique I use, where I squeeze a lemon under his nose and the oil from the lemon's skin perks up his olfactory bulb."

"Where is the bulb? Right there in his nose?"

"No, in his brain. So it makes his brain work better."

"Do you really think it helps?" Jodie asks, as they both hover over Dad in the living room.

"See? Squeeze, stimulate. And that makes his brain better."

"I can't believe something like that could really work."

"Maybe I'll let you try it sometime after I show you the proper technique."

"I don't know if I want to."

I'm waiting next to Dad with the newspaper that was just delivered, so we can start the crossword puzzle.

"Why are you here again, Jodie?" I ask.

"What do you mean?" A piece of hair with a purple barrette falls in front of Jodie's eyes, and she bats it back against her freckles.

"You were here yesterday, too. Don't you have anywhere else to go?"

"I wanted to come over and help Linda."

"Help her with what? She doesn't even do anything other than juice a lemon once in a while. I'm the one with all the responsibility here."

"You don't seem to me like you're doing all that much."

"I am. I have a very ambitious program going on here."

"I didn't mean to upset you, Billy."

"I'm not upset. We just have stuff to do right now. Just keep your opinions to yourself, okay?"

CITRUS CITY

Linda has gotten the idea that Dad would benefit more from constant stimulation of his olfactory bulb than from separate wafts of lemon oil or fresh lemon, so she comes home with a small lemon candle from the Dollar Store, which she and Jodie light in the living room near where Dad and I are playing cards.

"No you don't," I say.

"No I don't what?"

"Somebody's going to knock that over and cause a fire. Candles are for two things, Linda: churches and birthdays. Do you see either of those in this living room?"

"Stop trying to be such a big boss."

"Why do you think I have to be home day in, day out? Because I'm the only one with any sense around here. So put the candle out." I look at Dad's hand. He has three threes, and if he gets a fourth one he might be able to win. I try to remember how long ago one of us turned over a three.

"It won't fall over. It's in a votive glass. And what about Dad? He has lots of sense."

"That's not what I meant, and you know it. Now put the candle out, and don't start me arguing in front of Dad. It just upsets him."

"Dad's doing better. He slept for two hours last night. That's because of my upping the lemons." She balls up the wrapper from the candle and puts it in the pocket of Grandpa's overalls.

"Why do you two always fight so much?" Jodie asks.

Dad gets up and starts pacing again. "That's a good question," he says.

"Always?" I say. "Oh, I thought you were saying your own name, Always. Because you're Always Here!"

"Why are you getting so angry again?"

"Look, Jodie, we're under a lot of stress in this house. I don't think you realize that we have some very serious problems going on with my father's health. I don't know if I need to talk to your mother or what I need to do, but we have to arrange for you to not be here so often."

"I like having her here," Linda says. "She makes me feel better."

I put away the cards and go into the den to see what's

on TV. Dad stops pacing when he sees Michelle Kwan in a figure-skating competition. So the four of us watch that with the sound off. Jodie says Michelle is like a soul dancing. I like Michelle's triumphant yet humble openmouthed smile.

TREATMENT REPORT: DAY 69

Mom has been using jumbo shrimp as the seafood choice, and Dad is happy that something he likes, something he used to order when we went to a restaurant, is on the program. Mom has been cooking the shrimp with extra garlic, per E. Sutter, and we all eat the shells and the tails, too.

Last night Dad had an unbelievable sleep performance of four hours. This means he is finally getting better. I spent all day in school wondering what's causing this improvement, so we can build on it. Could it be Michelle? The shrimp? The calisthenics? Could the candle really be doing something? I've noticed that Dad may be getting bored by the affirmations, so maybe I should pick a single really good one. "We are one"?

After weeks of feeling sleepy in school, I'm beginning to feel more alert. Linda and I both believe that the special foods are improving our brain function.

We did it. We've turned it around.

TREATMENT REPORT: DAY 71

Dad has stopped eating shrimp because he says they remind him of curled-up babies. Mom offered him sardines instead, but he says they look like corpses stacked up in a concentration camp. The past couple of days he has eaten only a forkful or two of four of the brain foods, so he also has to take vitamins and supplements in pill form. But then, once in a while, he gets a craving for nuts.

Linda is gloating. Yesterday she ramped up the aromatherapy by going from one candle to two, each the size of a drinking glass. Then a girl at school who normally doesn't talk to me asked, "Bob, why are you wearing insect repellent in the winter?" When I asked Mom if we could stop using the candles some of the time, she said no. But are they doing any good? Is Mom backing Linda up only to make Linda feel she's contributing something?

Dad was awake the past two nights and very agitated. Mom stays up as long as she can but sometimes asks me to take over at two or three a.m. so she can nap. I walk Dad around the house, sometimes saying affirmations at the same time. I no longer can be sure if anything's helping, but I don't know if I should say anything to Mom. Maybe it would make more sense to continue as we are for a few more days, just in case the situation breaks. When Dad started on meds, the doctor said the chemicals had to build up in his system. Maybe it's the same with the food, the light, and the other cures.

PAPYRUS

"What's all this?"

"We're mashing up leaves."

"Why."

"We're going to make paper."

So this is Linda's revenge. Shredded brown stuff, pulpy and stemmy, lies in a puddle of tea-colored water in the bathtub. Linda is using the potato masher, and Jodie has the wooden thing you use to pound meat—a mallet, I guess it's called.

"Get this mess out of here. I'm not running a day-care service, you know."

"This isn't a mess," Linda says. "It's a worthwhile endeavor."

"You never have any fun," Jodie says. "Is that why you're mad?"

"No, it's because every time I open a door, you're behind it."

"Do you want to make paper with us?"

Mom had to go in for a special meeting at her office yesterday morning. Pudge was pressuring her to name a date when "all this" would be over and things at Brooksbie would get back to normal. I had to wait for Marty to show up at the house before I could leave for school. Then Mom was enraged at my allowing Dad to sit in front of the light box, between my watch and Marty's watch, a total of two hours. She said he will have to skip the light box for a few days because she thinks it's dangerous. I said I thought that was a mistake, even though deep down I'm not sure it's doing any good. And of course we had to pretend everything was okay, because we were talking in front of Dad.

When I managed to get Mom out of the room, I told her that I couldn't meet my family obligations if Jodie was going to be over all the time, that I would have to be paid for babysitting. "I'll take care of Dad," I said. "I'll even take care of Linda. But I won't take care of Jodie."

TREATMENT REPORT: DAY 75

Dad went back on the light box today, starting small with
ten minutes. I could have pushed to do more, but oh, well.
He skipped it entirely for a few days because Mom thought
he had had a light box overdose. He seems tired, so we're
scaling back on both the affirmations and the calisthenics.

Most days he has been eating just a few forkfuls of the
brain foods and maybe some nuts and a yogurt. But Mom
thinks it's important for him to get his seafood component
so his brain functioning will improve. She offered him
either tuna salad or crabmeat salad, but he wouldn't eat it.
Then she asked if he would eat lobster if she bought it, but
he said no, so she isn't spending the money. He lost a lot
of weight last week. Would it be better for him to eat just
anything to keep his strength up (as Jodie originally said)?

I told Linda I couldn't stand the candles anymore and
demanded that she remove them. Complained about it to
Mom, who sided with L.

POISSON/POISON

At dinner Linda and I are sitting at the table, eating our cooked salad. Dad has eaten only a small bowl of strawberries and is standing behind his chair. Jodie is miraculously absent.

"That's not enough," Mom tells him. "Remember? You have to have some seafood every day."

"I can't eat any more," Dad says. "I'm full."

She already told him yesterday that if he doesn't eat seafood he will have to take a drink of fish oil. She rustles a paper bag on the counter and comes back with a small cocktail glass.

"You have to drink this," Mom says.

"Does it taste bad?" Dad asks.

"No," Mom says, and she takes a sip from it. "Look, I'm doing it." Then she starts to cry.

"Are you lying to me, Adele?" Dad asks her.

"No," she says, and she starts crying again.

Then she leaves the glass on the table and goes to her room to get ready for bed. I pick up the glass. Linda and I both sniff it. It smells terrible. Mom stays in her room with the door closed, Dad is agitated, and I walk him around all night.

A DISTANT SHORE

A mouthful of steak-and-cheese challenges my jaw. The cheese forms a white glaze over knots of shaved meat. Bubbles of fat pop against the roof of my mouth. My mandibles ache. This is not a dream.

I whisk inadequate napkins one after the other from a dispenser to absorb the grease. "Another one?" Gordy asks.

I say no, still chewing, and chase the meat with black cherry soda that rinses clean and dry, almost salty.

Gordy finishes his soda, and the door of the sandwich shop pulls closed behind us on a spring. Sand washes across the threshold and rubs the soles of my sneakers.

"I'll pay you back sometime."

Gordy shrugs. "Forget it."

We walk down the road to a beach. A recent sleetstorm has left pockmarks in the sand, and the tide has gone out, leaving patterns like dragged hands in the wet areas, Vs within Vs within Vs. Our shadows walk with us dully.

Everything on this beach seems humanish to me. The moon, already visible at four p.m., resembles a fingernail clipping, and the fallen shreds of curly brown and black seaweed are snips from a giant's beard.

"What a great place." The beach is right near Gordy's house. It might even be a private beach. Once again it strikes me that everything about Gordy seems excellent. He's one of those preppy, well-rounded types and will probably be way more successful than me.

"Do your parents have a boat?" I ask.

"My dad has a modified lobster boat. It's in the marina for the winter."

Crap. I said "your parents" instead of "your father."

"We go out fishing for the weekend once in a while. Maybe you'd like to go with us sometime?"

On the spectrum of moronic things to say, asking about someone's dead parent as if they are still living is probably at the far end. How could I do this? Gordy's mother died shortly after they moved to town, of cystic fibrosis. People were talking about him when they first got here, because when his mother brought him in to register for school, she kept spitting blood into a handkerchief, right in the administrative office.

"Sorry. I forgot about your mom. Stupid."

"That's okay. It's not as bad anymore. She spent the whole last year talking to me about what to expect. That part was harder than it is now."

Then he surprises me by tossing an imaginary Frisbee. I catch the Frisbee and set the figures in my mind on it—the mother and father, little kitchen figures, diorama-like. I set them on it and whirl them out to sea, on their problem-plate, their Thought-Frisbee.

I walked out again! I walked out and left Linda in charge! Linda and Jodie are in charge of Dad. If Lucky Linda knows so much about what he needs, and Jodie is so indispensable, they will do a fine job taking care of him. I don't know whether Linda will tell Mom or not.

A barge heading into the harbor makes an engining thrum that carries. Gordy and I race to the end of the beach, where a copper-colored granite shelf is ideal for sitting but sends cold through the seat of my pants. At our backs is a stone wall. Above it, trees have twisted into tough survivalist shapes.

Gordy pulls a knit cap from his coat pocket. "Can you picture me out here this summer, maybe on the Fourth of July, with Brenda Mason or some other girl? I would have a blanket all spread out, maybe a portable grill. We'd be watching the fireworks over the harbor. You could come out too. Maybe it could be a double date. Who would you bring?"

Out on the water, the barge has cut its motor and a tugboat aligns itself behind it.

Is there anyone I can want? The prettiest girl I know is Lisa Melman, but she's in Linda's grade, and anyway, she's not as nice as her mother.

"I'm trying not to think too much about that stuff now. I'm trying to stay—I can't think of a better word—pure."

"Pure with girls?" Gordy asks.

"No, pure with thinking about only one thing at a time."

The tugboat, pushing, and the barge, gliding, are little and big, like the two-space and the five-space boats in the Battleship game. Concrete thoughts of chores to be done at home soften and rise. Mists, wishes, smoke signals. *I'm not there. I'm here now.* I got away.

"How is your dad, by the way?"

What to say? I brush the powdery sand into arcs with one hand.

"He's much better."

"That's great."

"What was wrong with him, anyway?"

"He was depressed."

"That must have been rough. He seems like a great guy."

"He really is."

"Glad to know he's better, then."

I rub my palms together slowly and watch the grains fall. "It takes a while to get better in a really obvious way that you would see by looking at him or talking to him, but things are getting better . . . underneath. It's more like an improvement in a different layer. An unconscious or subconscious layer."

"The human mind is fascinating, isn't it?" Gordy says. "I've always wondered about stuff like that."

"He'll probably be fully recovered soon. Maybe you can come by the house again."

"That would be great."

We're both lying back now, watching scuds of clouds move in to smother the moon.

"Do you want to get an ice cream or anything?"

"No, thanks. The sandwiches were enough. I should go home soon. I left without charging my headlight."

An arm of land reaches around the harbor. Across the water from us is a castle built by an eccentric inventor. It contains all kinds of things he lifted from humble little towns in Europe. A pipe organ, a reflecting pool of blue tile, even the coffin of a young girl. At the edge of the horizon, lights fall slowly from the sky—not shooting stars, but airplanes making their descent into Logan.

"Right after my mom died," Gordy says, "I would sit and look out here. Not toward Boston, but past it, where you could just keep going. I would try to convince myself that if I went far enough there was a place where we could all still be together."

"I know."

The sky darkens, but we lie on the rock like sacrifices. Then rain comes, hitting our faces like a metaphor.

TREATMENT REPORT: DAY 77

Dad refused to take his vitamins and supplements because he thought they might be unsafe. Mom was upset that he didn't trust her, and she is still getting over the fish oil incident. She bought some nutrient milkshakes in small cans, and Dad agreed to drink one.

A THREAT

Mom is at the supermarket. I tell Linda that the lemon candles are driving me berserk and that if she does not remove them I will tear a hole in her plush Garfield and stuff the candles inside. We're in her room, and I'm holding the Garfield and a pair of scissors. She leaps. We scuffle (quietly). We stop scuffling as Dad shuffles by.

Linda looks in a book Mom bought and calls Jodie, who comes over with two new lavender candles from the drugstore, each the size of a coffee can. Linda explains to Jodie the healing properties of the new candle scent.

I tell her the new candles are perfumey, cloying, and sickly sweet and I am sure Dad would feel the same, but she says too bad. She threatened two days ago to tell Mom about my leaving the house but has not done so yet. Jodie says I am a bad brother. It's obvious from Mom's expression when she gets home that she's noticed the new candles, but she doesn't say anything.

TREATMENT REPORT: DAY 81

Yesterday Dad ate nothing but two nutrient shakes and his pomegranate seeds. He slept well for a couple of hours, though.

Then tonight, Dad got a craving for vanilla ice cream, possibly stimulated by his recent experience with fake milkshakes.

"You really want ice cream?" Mom said. "I guess it's all right, but I want you to have fruit and nuts with it." She looked happy.

Linda and Jodie walked down to the nearby ice-cream place and brought back a quart of vanilla and some bananas and walnuts. Dad ate one and a half bowls, and Jodie commented that we looked just like a normal family. Dad actually smiled at Jodie. Mom smiled a lot then and danced Dad around the living room during calisthenics. Then Linda installed a third lavender candle in the bathroom, and no amount of towel-rubbing can get the stench off my body.

Why did Dad sleep for two hours last night? No one knows.

Why did he smile and eat ice cream? No one knows.

Do you hear that sound? It's the treatment team whistling in the dark.

A SYMBIOTIC RELATIONSHIP

Linda and Jodie have taken up calligraphy and are leaving ink everywhere. They are trying to get Dad to join them, even though occupational therapy is my treatment area.

"Linda," I tell her right in front of her friend, "Jodie has a home. It would be okay to leave her there sometimes."

The three of us were supposed to be the treatment team, Mom said. We were going to take care of Dad as a family. So why *is* she always here? Jodie seems to have no existence outside of being my sister's friend. It's like Linda is a slide projector and Jodie is a slide. If Linda were to die suddenly, Jodie would die at the same instant, of the same illness. Even if they were on opposite sides of the world.

TREATMENT REPORT: DAY 83

Yesterday Dad had one nutrient shake and a dish of ice cream, and M. told him no more ice cream until he ate some of his brain foods, but then she let him have another bowl because he looked so skinny.

Then he had another bad night, so we took turns staying up with him. Linda did a couple of hours, and I'm sure Jodie would have too if she'd been allowed to stay. Mom kept asking him questions. Wasn't he feeling good the day before? What went wrong? Of course he can't answer this. What's he going to say?

BREWING

Dad has had another bad night and day. At suppertime, Mom starts fixing the cooked salad and navy beans while Dad paces the other end of the house.

"Is Jodie gone? Is Linda ready for dinner?" she asks.

"I don't know." Reading some additional library info in the living room, I rattle the photocopies loudly so she'll know she's interrupted me.

"Well, could you call her?"

"I'll call her in a few minutes. I just want to finish this article."

"Oh, you're no help," she says over the room divider.

I put my article down and go into the kitchen. "I'm no help?" I repeat.

"Go on. Go back to what you were doing. I'll call her myself." She waves a pot holder dismissively.

"Linda!" I shout without leaving the kitchen. "Supper!"

"Billy."

I put my hands in my pockets and raise my shoulders. "You just said I was no help. What exactly did you mean by that?"

"I didn't mean anything. I'm tired, okay?"

"No help with Dad? I'm no help with Dad?"

"Just forget it." Mom turns down the heat under the bean pot, then removes the jar of brewer's yeast from the cabinet and checks the label.

"What other help do you have? I'm it. I'm the help."

"I'm going to have to try something else," she says in a low voice. "I'll look in my books again after supper. I don't understand why he has good days and bad days, but overall—so far, anyway—he's not getting any better."

Linda comes into the kitchen and opens the silverware drawer to start setting the table. "Have you thought about starting Dad on yoga, Mom? Jodie's mother says it's very centering."

"That sounds worthwhile, Linda. Can you find out a little more about it?"

"Of course he's not any better!" I snap. "He's not getting better because we keep changing the treatments!"

My voice fills our small house. Dad comes in from his bedroom.

"Son . . . ," he begins, laying his hand on my arm.

"We can't start him on yoga now! There are already too many variables! How are we going to know what's working?"

"Too many variables?" Mom repeats.

"Variables! They're the things that change! Constants are the things that stay the same! You keep the constants the same and then you test the variables! You don't start five or six treatments at once and have them all overlapping! You use the scientific method! You only test one variable at a time! You pick one and you test it!"

"You don't have to explain the scientific method. I know what variables are. You don't have to explain anything to me." Mom clutches the yeast jar with both hands, like a little kid. "I thought we decided it would be best to try everything we could."

"Please don't argue," Dad says, looking at his hands, flexing them.

"Well, obviously it's not best! We're not accomplishing anything! We have to start over, and this time use the scientific method! Just start all over, from scratch, and try the treatments one at a time."

Linda dumps the utensils in a tangle on the table. "Can't

you keep your voice down, Billy? Look how upset Dad is getting."

"But we will have lost all these weeks," Mom says.

"You can't look at it that way. If you really cared about Dad you would take what I'm saying seriously."

"Take it seriously!" Mom snaps. "I'm not taking this seriously?"

"Things were getting better, Billy," Linda says. "They were. We just have to figure out why. We just have to figure out what to do next. Why don't you lighten up on Mom—she's really stressed."

Dad goes to the stove and puts one arm around Mom.

"Son," he orders faintly, "apologize to your mother." He's trying to be the old peacemaker Dad, but it comes off like an echo of an echo. A photocopy of a photocopy.

"But I'm right, Dad," I plead. "You know I'm right."

Mom's face looks soft and somehow dented.

"Apologize to your mother, Billy."

"I'm sorry."

"You don't sound very sorry."

"Say it like you mean it," Mom says.

"No."

"I'm sorry to you, Dad." I touch his arm briefly, the

red hairs there that I also have. "I'm just not that sorry to Mom."

"I can't take this," says Dad. He leaves the kitchen to pace and rub his arms.

I go to my room and throw on my coat and shoes. I wheel Triumph across the living-room carpet. I leave a nice thick line of soil and sand.

MONSTER

"Can I come in?"

"Sure. *Mi casa* . . . Wow. You don't look good," Gordy says.

He doesn't look good either. He's wearing sweats and white socks, and his face seems puffy and strange. Through the doorway comes the music of a brass band, turned up to a high volume.

"I'm sorry. Is this a bad time to stop by?"

"No, it's okay. I'd just as soon not sit around by myself." He steps aside and turns down the stereo until it is merely loud. I drop onto the couch with my coat on. Inside my chest, something thin and gray and hollow as a used light-bulb is finally breaking.

"I hate to repeat myself, but you really don't look good," Gordy repeats. "When was the last time you got any sleep?"

"He's not getting any better."

"He's not? But you thought he was, didn't you?"

"Well, he's not." I press both sets of fingertips into my closed eyes.

"You don't look right. Do you need something to eat?"

"No. In fact, I might prefer to throw up."

Gordy goes into the kitchen and comes back with a bottle of blue Gatorade and two of the largest-size beef jerky sticks.

"Here." He opens my left hand and slaps a sausage stick into it. "Bathroom's down there." He points along a hall.

I let the hand drop into my lap. Gordy peels the wrapper halfway and slaps it into my palm again. "Take at least a few bites. When you're done eating, you can stretch out and take a nap on the couch."

"Where's your dad?"

"He's working. He usually is. Don't worry, you're not disturbing anything."

"I can't sleep now," I tell him. "I shouldn't even stay."

"Do your parents know where you are? Do you want me to call them?"

"No, don't do that. Let them wonder. Let them wonder where I am." I picture Mom, that tiny faraway holographic Mom, getting along without me. We could abandon one another.

"I'll tell them you're staying here for a few hours."

"No, I won't stay." I tear off a bit of the leathery jerky. "I just needed to get out for a while."

Gordy opens a bottle of blue Gatorade for himself. "So your dad isn't any better?"

"No."

"Is he worse?"

"He might be."

"Is there anything I can do?"

"I don't know what the next step should be. If I knew, I would do it myself."

Once I've finished both jerky sticks and drunk some of the Gatorade, Gordy brings me a pillow and a New England Patriots blanket. I push my sneakers off toe to heel. The room is painted dark green, with a grandfather clock and glass-front cases filled with old books. On the stereo, a solitary drum taps like a heartbeat. After a signal from the cornet, the band begins "Just a Closer Walk with Thee." But the sound is slow, screeching, and loopy, not like church music, from any church I've been to at least. It sounds drunk and dizzy, like the soundtrack of an ancient cartoon. The musicians veer off in different directions with no unison in pitch or timing. Like some grief has set them loose and cursed them to wander.

When I close my eyes, pictures are there, of a brass band in black suits, a hole in the ground with my mother and Linda standing beside it. Where am I? I'm playing in the band. But I won't cry. I won't cry yet.

When I open my eyes again, the sad music is over. I sit up and push the blankets aside. The band is playing "Oh, Lady, Be Good," swingy and brash with curlicues of improvisation. Gordy is waiting in the doorway, having changed into khakis and a sweater.

"How long did I sleep?" I ask him.

"About an hour. Let's go do something."

"I should get home."

"Have you done anything remotely fun since Boston?"

"Fun? *No comprende* 'fun.'" I dig under the blanket for my coat. "I need to get home. Thanks for the break."

"Let's go to the arcade for an hour." He hands me the cell phone. "You can call your parents and tell them where you're going."

"Nope. Thanks."

"Too bad—I'm kidnapping you," Gordy says, getting his parka from the hall closet. "Call the cops if you want to. We're going."

We walk half a mile along the shoreline. The low tide

smells like the fish oil Mom tried to give Dad. The sky hangs cold and black, fingered with gray where clouds have been.

The arcade is a creaky wooden building that once had a carousel, nickelodeons, and other little-kid amusements. My parents had brought me here to play Skee-Ball, watch cartoons in a machine for a nickel, or pay a puppet fortune-teller a dime to wave her arms over a crystal ball and spit out my fortune. After a while someone caught on that the whole operation was too cheap. They sold the old amusements and put in carpeting and overhead TVs and much newer games that cost fifty cents or a dollar. I begged and begged my parents to take me to the place they now called A Big Waste of Money.

Gordy slides ten dollars into a change machine. He dips his hand twice into the mouthful of quarters and hands me some. The air is thick with electronic shooting sounds—*voot, voot*—and the voices of synthetic race announcers. Bells mark a hundred microsuccesses, important in the moment but quickly forgotten.

Gordy stacks quarters on the counter to reserve a turn on the Dethbord, a skateboard simulator that has a safety bar on four sides and orange warnings all over it. We watch the current player, a boy younger than us, nearly fall over as the board approaches, at high speed, a pit of flames. He seems surprised when the skateboard on the video screen starts to fall away from his feet, first skidding forward without him, then twirling downward like something running down a drain, getting smaller and smaller. He collapses against the handrail. Heartbreaking.

"Hunker down!" Gordy shouts to him. "Reach for the board!"

I drop two quarters into a game that involves tossing small plush animals—possibly prizes left over from the old arcade—into the gullet of an animatronic figure that looks sort of like a man but is covered with hair and has scary green eyes. The monster breaks through a gate toward me, bellowing, as soon as my second quarter lands in the coin-box. I toss a buck-toothed beaver in a construction hat, then a brown teddy bear with a patchwork heart, and then a yellow kitten in a square-dancing dress. The animation is so lifelike that you can see muscles moving under the monster's skin, and each time a cute little animal goes down the monster's throat, the bellows are interspersed with a high-pitched scream like a baby falling out a window, and the panicky shouts of helpless townspeople.

By the third round of the game I feel jumpy and robotic. The hundred points per cute stuffed animal makes me feel guilty, but I don't want the monster to bellow all the way down his platform to me. So I lob and lob, reacting only to the advancing monster and the beeps of the electronic scoreboard, blocking out the pathetic cries of the little prizes: 6100, 6200—*Eeee! Eeee!* Then I hear Gordy hollering. I wonder, is he in trouble too? I lob a pink snail with a rainbow-striped shell and big sunglasses, then glance over my shoulder until I see him, attracting a crowd around his stint on the skateboard. Turning back to my game, I see Mitchell at the pinball machines, with Andy.

Mitchell has been lobbying to come over, or to have me to his house, for the past two and a half months. "I don't know what you did to get grounded on this scale," he said a few days ago, "but I hope it was fun." That was his parting shot, I guess, since he has stopped asking.

Now Andy notices me, but Mitchell hasn't. I reach into the bin of small plush animals while watching Mitchell over my shoulder, and the bin feels empty. I see that the monster is only two feet away; if I don't weave or duck he could graze me with the horrible black nails on his subhuman, flailing hands. Having missed the last few throws, I've been punished with an empty bin. My score disappears and an electronic display flashes: WHAT WILL YOU DO NOW?

I leave my game to go and yank on Gordy's jacket. He has begun another round on the skateboard, several feet above a cheering crowd of girls, kiddies, and moms.

"We have to go!" I tell him. "It's late!"

Gordy turns his head for a second. "Not now! I'm in the Seventh Circle!"

Across the room, Andy is telling Mitchell something and pointing toward the plush-animal game. Mitchell starts looking around.

"I'm going now, with or without you."

Gordy hops down. He picks one little kid from the crowd.

"You, little fella. You can finish this game," he tells the boy.

"You mean it?"

"I'm going!" I tell Gordy. I break into a run.

We're almost out of the arcade, but Gordy looks back at the last moment. "Hey. Did you see who's here?"

"Wait a minute, you guys," Andy calls out.

They catch up to us between the customer service stand and the lost children booth.

"Oh, hey, Gordy, Morrison," Mitchell says. "Morrison, I thought you weren't allowed out except to go to school. I thought you were grounded or something."

"Hi, Mitchell. How was your score?"

"The hell with that, okay? You said you weren't allowed out. I've known you since birth, practically. You could just tell me if you didn't feel like getting together."

"I'm having some problems, okay? Some personal problems. I can't really talk about it right now."

"Then why are you here?"

"I made him come with me," Gordy says. "I kidnapped him. Really."

"Why can't you leave the house?"

"All I can tell you is, any time I'm not at home, I feel sort of sick and lousy."

"That doesn't sound good," Andy says. "Are you getting that disease where people are afraid to leave their houses? I think it's called acrophobia."

"Agoraphobia," Mitchell corrects him, keeping his eyes on me. "Well, don't expect me to ask you to do anything again. Don't hold your breath about hearing from me, period."

"It's my fault," Gordy says as we walk past the beach

again. "I shouldn't have pushed you into it. I thought you might feel better if you had a change of location. When my mom was sick, I always got an energy boost if I went out once in a while."

Back at Gordy's, I retrieve Triumph from a stone archway leading to the front steps. It's one of the few times I've left the bike without the Kryptonite lock, and I have to make sure I don't do this again. Starting out, my headlamp is weak too—the battery could get permanently drained. I can't let this happen again, that I stop thinking and just let things go. If I can't manage myself, how can I help anyone else?

Must get home, must get home, I chant. I burst into a sprint at the bottom of our hill. The sound of my wheels brings Mom and Dad to the picture window. They're already in their bathrobes. Their silhouettes are dark against the bright glass, like two lighthouses in negative, and I open the door.

Mom tried to reprimand me for running out like that, but since she had been home at the moment and I had no specific responsibilities at the time, her complaint slid through my head without gaining traction.

"But you really upset your father," she said. She said it's disturbing for Dad to hear us fighting with one another, and we all have to be really careful not to argue in front of him.

A FRIENDLY VISIT

The doorbell rings and it's June. Not the month of June, but June from Dad's office.

"Hi, sweetie!" June says when Mom opens the door. "How are things?"

Mom looks like someone has squeezed three drops of water inside the back of her collar with an eyedropper. June begins to reach toward Mom for a hug, then, thinking better of it, puts one hand back on the doorknob. She's carrying a paper cone of white carnations.

"I'm sorry, June," Mom says, "but this isn't a good time. I was just doing the dishes."

"Oh, do you want some help?" June asks. "I'll do anything you haven't had time to do, including wiping out unidentifiable green liquefied substances that may have congealed on your refrigerator shelves. Just toss me a pair of rubber gloves and put me to work."

"Hello, Mrs. Melman." June is wearing a sweater and

pants in the palest shade of pink, the color of rose petals.

"Billy, honey, are you doing all right?"

"Not too bad. I guess we're all a little tired and worn out." I feel like collapsing against her and breathing in those roses.

"Who is it?" Dad asks from the bedroom.

"It's June!" June sings over Mom's head, at the very moment that Mom mutters, "It's June" at the lowest end of her register, so the two of them sound like a woman and a man performing a duet.

Dad comes into the living room.

"Hi, Bill," June says softly. She intertwines her free hand in Dad's and hangs there with him for a minute, standing with her head down the same way he does. "Everyone says hello. They are counting the days until your return. We don't have anyone to play 'Guess That Opera' with us anymore. It's a very quiet place these days."

She turns to Mom. "May I put these in water, Adele?"

"I'll do it." Mom walks briskly to June and removes the carnations from her hand.

"Let's sit down for a minute, Bill, and I'll bore you with all the current office problems. The whole sorry state of things. You know, Adele, I'd be glad to cover for a while if you need a break. Why don't you take a rest, go out and see a movie or something, and I'll stay here? Lisa's at a friend's house, but I can have her get dropped off here when she's done. Is Linda home? The bunch of us will order Chinese or something."

Despite my reluctance to leave Mrs. Melman, I go into the kitchen to see what Mom wants to do. Filling a vase with water, Mom stares stonily out the kitchen window at the darkened backyard. "Typical, typical June," she says to me in a low voice. "No sense of the situation. I can't believe she didn't call first." Another drop rolls down Mom's spine.

Mom returns to the living room with the vase. Her back is rigid.

"June," she says finally. "Have you noticed that Bill is not quite himself? Don't you see that he's not behaving as usual? Do you even notice that you're talking to him and he's not answering you?"

"I'm sorry, June," Dad says, not meeting her eyes but ruffling the tips of the white carnations in the vase, until the petals are bent and brownish. "That's right. I'm not feeling well."

"That's all right, Bill," June says, still sitting on the

couch beside Dad. "I know you're not well. That's why I'm here. Adele, I didn't stop by expecting anyone to entertain me. I didn't expect a big cocktail party when I showed up unannounced. I didn't expect a lot of laughs. Just a short, pleasant visit, to check up on you and see if you need anything, to say everyone at Liberty Fixtures is thinking of you two. Today I entertain you; another day, when I need entertaining, you'll entertain me, right? That's how it goes. That's a corny old practice that some call friendship."

"June—Mrs. Melman," I interrupt. I'm standing in the living room near Dad. Mom and I thought we sent a clear signal by not sitting down. "I'm sure Dad appreciates your visit, but we haven't been in that type of situation for a while. We don't want anyone to entertain us."

"We're just trying to get through the day here," Mom adds. "Doing the bare minimum that needs to be done. Getting up in the morning and trying to eat a meal. Putting one foot in front of the other. Trying to make it from Monday to Tuesday to Wednesday."

June stands, smoothing her sweater and slacks. "Are you saying you don't want me to come back? Should I tell everyone at Liberty not to come?"

Mom shrugs—let June draw her own conclusions.

"There's a lot of suffering in this house," she says, so low you can barely hear.

"Why suffer alone?" June says. "Why not share it? I just came from tennis—my brain is flooded with endorphins. I was singing in the car on the way over here. I can stand a little of someone else's suffering."

"Thanks for these, June," Dad whispers, pointing to the flowers.

"Do you want me to phone, is that it? May I visit again if I phone first?"

"We'll see you at the bat mitzvah when the time comes," Mom says to her.

"Adele . . ." June widens her eyes and shakes her head, as if this will help her understand better. "Do you need anything from the supermarket?"

Mom swings her head—no.

"All right, Bill," June says. "I'll see you back at work . . . soon, I hope." Dad is sitting on the couch, nervously ruffling the flowers. June squeezes his shoulder, winks and smiles at me. Then, at the door, she hugs Mom more tightly and for longer than anyone expects.

IN PRIVATE

A man and a woman kneel beside their bed. He wears a tired pair of geometrically printed pajamas, and she wears a white kimono with gray at the edge of the sleeves. Their heads are bowed, their hands folded. She speaks for both of them, in a low, unassuming voice.

Dad has always called himself an agnostic, saying he does not know whether there's a God, and cannot know, but that if there is a God, then that God is most likely an all-knowing, understanding God who will understand why Dad might not believe in Him. That Dad's older child has attempted to cover his bases in the same manner is disappointing to Dad. Because Dad seems to think, or did once think, that the larger the number of believers in the family, the greater the chance that the entire family would be saved. Or if "saved" is too strong a word, the greater the chance that the entire family would be entitled to whatever Treats are in store when this candy store is closed for business—

eternal life being the ultimate, of course, and forgiveness being nothing to sneeze at either. Dad has also hoped that one believer, one very strong believer—Mom—will produce enough salvational energy to carry him to Heaven on her coattails if necessary, so he won't miss anything.

But for now, these philosophical questions must be put aside. For now, Mom must speak for both of them, because over the past two weeks Dad has gradually stopped speaking. He sits with us at mealtimes, still getting up to pace, he watches the painting show with a slight smile on his face, and it's hard to know whether he thinks the show is pleasant or whether he is sneering at the whole endeavor of painting. He might say a few words—"yes," "no," "it's on the nightstand"—but he no longer initiates communication, and he shares nearly nothing about his inner state. He seems to have put himself away, placed himself in another room for safety, while the him we see walks among us, acting convincing enough to distract us from the body in the closet.

Mom stops murmuring and shifts her position, and it looks like she's going to get up. But instead she positions herself behind Dad's shoulder and wraps her arms around him from the back. She clasps her hands around

Dad's hands like a parent helping a child to hold a pencil. She murmurs again with her cheek pressed to the cloth on Dad's back. Either she's showing him how to pray, or she's doing Dad's praying for him, transmitting from another station, faking God into thinking that the prayers are coming from him.

TREATMENT REPORT: DAY 89

Having stayed up with Dad for three nights, Mom doesn't have the energy for leading calisthenics or cooking special meals. Linda has her own interests. Investment in the multi-pronged treatment plan is at an all-time low. With my long-term doubts, I won't push to continue it.

Under the treatment plan we disagreed, but we worked as a team. Now our minds have chosen separate corners, like four strangers dividing the space in an elevator.

What is it that Dad finds when he hides in *his* inner room? That's what I want to know. Maybe it's some sadness that's stuck in there and isn't coming out, like the opposite of music.

THE VOICE

I remember an article I printed out at the library when Mom and I were doing our research. It's by Robert W. Firestone, from a 1986 issue of *Psychotherapy*.

> The voice refers to a system of negative thoughts about self and others that is antithetical to self. Our operational definition excludes those thought processes that are concerned with constructive planning, creative thinking, self-appraisal, fantasy, value judgments, and moral considerations. The voice is not an actual hallucination but an identifiable system of thoughts experienced much as an actual voice. The author feels that suicide is the ultimate conclusion of acting upon this negative thought process.
>
> The voice refers to a generalized hostile attitude toward self and as such is the language of an overall self-destructive process. It is an overlay of the

personality that is not natural, but learned or imposed from without. Although the voice may at times be related to one's value system or moral considerations, its statements against the self usually occur after the fact and tend to increase one's self-hatred rather than motivating one to alter behavior in a constructive fashion.

The voice becomes the core of a negative concept of self when it goes unchallenged. The process of "listening" to the voice predisposes an individual toward self-limiting behavior and negative consequences. In other words, people make their behavior correspond to the distorted negative perceptions they have of themselves. . . .

The voice operates along a continuum ranging from mild self-criticisms—thoughts that promote self-denying and self-limiting behavior—to vicious abuse or self-recriminations that are accompanied by intense rage and injunctions to injure oneself. . . .

Our clinical material indicated that a process of actual self-denial on a behavioral level parallels the voice attacks, and that this self-denial can lead to a cycle of serious pathology. As a person gradually retreats from seeking gratification of self in the real world of object relations, he or she becomes progressively indifferent to life. He or she tends to give up more and more areas of experience that were once found pleasurable and worthwhile. Actual self-harm is much more likely to be acted out after the individual has withdrawn his or her interest and affect from the external world and from an active pursuit of personal goals, a form of "social suicide."

THE CASE OF MIRIAM H.

This sends me back to a chapter from *Mind and Motivation* by Missy Bernard Welton:

> Miriam H. was a vibrant, talkative thirty-five-year-old who was building a successful career in finance. She enjoyed the lifestyle of a single young professional, with a large circle of friends and a variety of regular activities that included cooking classes and swing dancing. Several months before commencing treatment, however, she was passed over for a promotion at work. Shortly afterward, she served as a bridal attendant in the nuptials of a younger sister. These two events caused her to reevaluate her life, mostly in the form of a running internal critique of her own value and abilities. An interview with Miriam showed the progression of her self-critical thoughts:
>
> **Miriam:** I had this speech in my head, like a tape

recording. "You've been deluding yourself all this time. You thought things were okay, and they really weren't...."
It was as if my life were being lived behind a facade or a veil, and someone had lifted the veil off and I could see how ugly everything really was. . . . My happiness was an illusion, and now I was being shown the reality.

MBW: And the reality was . . . ?

Miriam: That I wasn't really valued the way I thought I should be. . . . That I had been kidding myself. People pretended to think a lot of me, but when push came to shove, there were a number of other people that were held up as superior. I was in a lower category, like, a lesser category. Something seemed to tell me that I should try to isolate myself as much as possible, and prepare, because those incidents were just the beginning, and the end was coming soon.

MBW: The end?

Miriam: That the end was coming, and that it would be a relief. That I could hurry it up. I was in control, you know? It was all up to me. And the more I hurried it up, the sooner I would be free.

Could this be why Dad has stopped communicating?

CONVERSATION #1

Me: Do you want anything to eat?

Dad: What?

Me: We're having dinner soon. Mom wants to know if you're hungry. We're having ham and potato salad from the deli. Either? Both?

Dad: No, thanks.

Me: Are you sure?

Dad: Yes.

Jodie: I think he wants to become a vegetarian. Is that it, Mr. Morrison? You want to become a vegetarian?

Me: He said no, Jodie.

Linda: You don't know anything about what Dad wants.

Mom: Please stop arguing.

Me: Hey, Lucky Linda, why don't *you* go eat dinner—animal, vegetable, or mineral? How about rocks? Why don't you try eating a great big rock so you finally shut up?

Dad: Sssssss.

Linda: You're upsetting him. See?

Me: Why don't you just go away?

Me: Okay, then. You're not hungry. Let me know if you change your mind.

Dad: All right.

Me: How about a game?

Dad: I don't think so. Not right now, anyway.

Me: Don't you want to do anything?

Dad: I'll just sit here. Quiet.

Me: Do you want company?

Dad: No.

Me: You like being by yourself?

Dad: Yes.

Me: Mind if I stick around?

Dad: Suit yourself.

Me: I'll stay, then.

Dad: All right.

Me: I wanted to see you. I worried about you during school today.

Dad: Can you be quiet?

Me: Sorry. I'll sit here quietly.

Me: Are you okay? You don't look too good.

Dad: Nothing new. Just the same.

Me: Something seems wrong.

Dad: Can you be quiet?

Me: Yes, I'll be quiet. I'll read.

Me: This is interesting.

Dad: Quiet?

Me: Sorry.

CONVERSATION #2

Mom: I'm going to bed. What about you?

Dad: I'll sit for a while.

Mom: Do you want to take a bath?

Linda: I have bubble bath, Dad. Do you want to take a bubble bath?

Dad: No, thanks.

Mom: You'll go as is, then?

Dad: Yes.

Me: I'll sit with you, Dad.

Dad: I'm all right.

Mom: Don't stay up too late.

Dad: Go to bed, son.

Me: I'm not tired. I'll sit quietly, I promise. I'll read.

Me: This is interesting.

Dad: Shhh.

Me: Dad, are you hearing some kind of voice?

Dad: I'm tired, son. Please go away.

Me: Dad, is the voice telling you not to talk to me?

CONVERSATION #3

Me: Dad. Mom's out, and you and I are going to have a little talk.

Dad: (Silence.)

Me: I know what's happening to you, see? I know all about it.

Dad: (Silence.)

Me: I don't know all about it—I didn't mean to say that. But I do know about it. I feel fairly confident.

Dad: (Silence.)

Me: I really don't like that expression on your face. It just isn't you.

Dad: (Silence.)

Me: Look at me, okay? Look toward me. Please.

Dad: (Silence.)

Me: Okay. Now, Dad. I want you to know that the comments you are about to hear are not directed at you. So please don't take any of them personally. They're directed at that voice you're hearing.

I repeat: This is not directed at you!

Dad:	(Silence.)
Me:	All right. . . . I'm going to exorcise you, you parasitic bastard!
Dad:	(Silence.)
Me:	I'm sorry, Dad. Could you possibly forgive me?
Dad:	(Silence.)
Me:	Look at me, please. Look right into my eyes.
Dad:	(Silence.)
Me:	Right in the eyes. Right here. Sorry.
Dad:	(Silence.)
Me:	Bastard! *Vamos!*
Dad:	(Silence.)
Me:	Don't you get it—you're not wanted! Get the hell out and leave him alone!
Dad:	(Silence.)
Jodie:	Here we are. My mom bought us all chicken nuggets.

TREATMENT REPORT: DAY 91

Why does Dad refuse to discuss the voice? Is he protecting the voice by not talking to me?

My best hope is to go in, way in, into what you might call enemy territory, and see if I can hear the voice myself.

CONVERSATION #4

Me: Hi, Dad.

Me: How's everything going?

Me: No need to answer me.

Me: I'm just going to sit here quietly and observe you. But don't be self-conscious. Pretend I'm not even here.

Dad: I'm so tired.

Me: I know you are. I heard you walking around last night. Now, I want you to just behave as you ordinarily do. Talk to your voice, or whatever. I think I have a pretty good handle on this, and I'm going to fill in the blanks for myself as best I can. So, begin whenever you're ready.

Dad: Why don't you go away and leave me alone?

Me: Was that addressed to me? I'm not going anywhere. Sorry.

Me: I can wait. I brought something to read.

Dad: (Silence.)

Me: As I said, it will be just as if I'm not here.

Me: (Silence.)

Dad: (Silence.)

Me: Proceed.

Dad: (More silence.)

Me: (Even more silence.)

Dad: God, I'm tired.

Voice in Dad's head: Of course you're tired. And you're not going to get any better. You're only going to get worse.

Me: (!!!)

Dad: I don't understand. . . .

Voice: Speak up! You're so slow all the time! Why don't you just say what you mean.

Dad: I don't understand how I got to be this way.

Voice: What way?

Dad: So tired like this. And unable to do anything. When I used to do so many things.

Voice: Like what?

Dad: Like—

Voice: Go ahead! Name them. So many, right? Go ahead and name even one!

Dad: I can't.

Voice: Why not, big shot?

Dad: Because I'm so tired.

Voice: You know, you think you're really something special, don't you? You think the world revolves around you, the sun rises and sets—

Dad: No, I don't.

Voice: Don't interrupt me when I'm talking! The sun rises and sets on your feeble head, doesn't it?

Dad: No, it doesn't. I never said that. See . . .

Voice: See what, blind man?

Dad: You know, you were wrong before. They do care about me.

Voice: Well, yeah. When you're sitting right in front of them. They're just pretending.

Dad: But if they're pretending in order to make me feel better . . . Doesn't that mean . . . ? Forget it—it's too complicated now.

Voice: How do you think they act when you're not around? If you went out for the day, how do you think they'd talk about you?

Dad: God, I'm tired.

Voice: Have you even thought about that?

Dad: I don't believe you. Enough.

Jodie: Can I play?

Me: We're not playing. Why don't you get out of here?

Linda: You can't tell Jodie what to do. Not anymore. We're all living in peace and harmony.

Jodie: Well, I thought you were playing a guessing game or something.

Me: Hold on there, Dad. It's nothing you two will understand.

LINDA

"You have to tell us," Linda says.

"Yes, tell us, Billy."

"You're not supposed to go off in your own direction and make up your own treatments. We're supposed to be a team, remember?" Linda insists.

I take Linda and Jodie into Linda's room and tell them what I've been working on. When Linda hears that I think Dad might have a voice in his head that could make him hurt himself, she doesn't start to blubber the way she did that first night, when we talked about the suicide movie. Instead, she looks completely calm.

"Okay, well, the most important thing," Linda says, "is that we not tell Mom about it. We have to take care of it ourselves, and not worry Mom with it, because she has too much going on and she couldn't handle it."

"Should we tell my mom?" Jodie asks. "She always knows what to do."

"Could she keep it to herself?" I ask.

"Probably not," Linda says.

"Then no."

"Then it's just us," Jodie says in a small voice.

CONVERSATION #5

Dad: Maybe I'll be able to get some sleep tonight.

Voice: Ha!

Dad: What?

Voice: How can you think you're going to sleep? You should know better by now.

Dad: There's a chance that I might sleep, isn't there? A little bit of a chance.

Mom: Bill, should we start getting ready for bed?

Dad: I don't think I want to go yet.

Mom: Why not? It's late.

Dad: I don't think I'll be able to sleep.

Mom: Well, you do have trouble sleeping most nights, but that doesn't mean you should stop trying. What about the little sleeping pills, Bill?

Dad: I don't want one.

Mom: Why not?

Dad: I'm afraid I'll get hooked.

Mom: Bill, honey, look at it. See—it's just a tiny, white, store-bought, over-the-counter, nonprescription, not even very powerful, little PILL!

Voice: What do you care? Take the whole bottle.

Dad: I'm not going to take it.

Mom: Honey, it's such a tiny pill. I'm sorry, I know I'm beginning to sound exasperated. *Mmmmmph-pheeww.* We won't let you get addicted, I promise. We'll monitor you. Billy, you'll help me monitor Dad so he doesn't get hooked, right?

Me: Sure. I love to monitor my parents. That way they're less likely to monitor me. Heh, heh. Just kidding, Dad. But seriously, Mom, I don't think Dad should be taking those if he doesn't want to. Isn't there something else he can do?

Dad: Could I only take a little piece of one?

Mom: I don't know if that would do any good.

Voice: Hell, take all of 'em! What do you care?

Dad: Maybe I'll take a little bit of it. A quarter of it.

Mom: All right, then. Take just a quarter if that's what you want to do. If you feel okay with that, maybe you'll want to increase later.

Dad: Okay. I'll take a quarter.

Mom:	Billy, cut this into quarters, will you?
Me:	This? Cut this into quarters? I'll do it, but I'm going to need an electron microscope. Are you sure we shouldn't just skip it?
Linda:	Maybe he should just skip it, Mom. Maybe he should take a bubble bath instead. Do you want some of my bubble bath, Dad? It makes you itchy afterward, but the bubbles are really big. Your entire body disappears under the bubbles. It's very relaxing.
Dad:	I don't think so.
Mom:	How about a shower?
Dad:	No, I guess not.
Mom:	So you'll go as is again, huh?
Dad:	Yep. Just as is. Just as I am.
Mom:	How are you doing with that sleeping pill, Billy?
Me:	I'm getting it. I'm using a razor blade. If it would just stay still long enough while I bear down . . . Unnh. That's halves. Wait a minute. Quarters coming up next.
Mom:	Try not to cut into the surface of the table. Or your hands, for that matter.
Me:	Okay. Here are your quarters. Are you sure you want him to have this if he doesn't want to?

Mom: Get that down. Water. Good.

Dad: Wait . . .

Voice: This could be just the beginning.

Mom: Did it taste all right?

Voice: Just the beginning.

Dad: I wish I hadn't taken it.

Mom: Did I pressure you too much? I didn't mean to pressure you.

Me: I don't think he wanted to take it. Maybe we shouldn't be giving those to him.

Linda: What about trying warm milk again? Isn't milk supposed to be good?

Dad: Cancel . . .

Voice: The beginning of the end.

LINDA'S DREAM

The next afternoon, while Dad's watching TV, Linda tells me that she had a bad dream, just as bad as Dad's with the metal box. In the dream, all of us were dead except for Dad, who was walking around outside. The rest of us had been lying for weeks inside the house with the door and windows sealed up, but Dad couldn't get to us and so there was no one to help him. Linda takes this as a sign that he is about to hurt himself soon, just like I said when describing the article. She says she needs to do something about it, she just doesn't know what. And we both agree not to tell Mom about the dream.

CONVERSATION #6

Mom: What are you two doing over there? I'm hearing an awful lot of quiet.

Me: I'm doing a sort of quiet meditation with Dad. Sort of an hypnosis.

Mom: An hypnosis? Do you mean *a* hypnosis?

Me: Whatever.

Mom: Well, is it working?

Me: I think so. We're concentrating very hard right now.

Voice: He doesn't need you. I'm the one he needs.

Me: That's ridiculous.

Voice: I'll tell you what's ridiculous, or should I say who.

Me: I'm ridiculous?

Voice: You already know that, don't you? You're going to lose him.

Me: No.

Voice: Can you wave good-bye? Wave good-bye, Billy! Wave good-bye to Daddy!

Me:	You are a parasitic leech that serves no human purpose whatsoever, and you should be going now.
Voice:	No human purpose! I offer him the Biggie.
Me:	What's that? What's the Biggie?
Voice:	Relief.
Me:	I offer that. Mom and Linda and I do.
Voice:	Oh yeah, how?
Me:	We do all kinds of things.
Voice:	I can read your mind, you know. I know you realize you're full of it.
Me:	That's it. I'm done with you.
Voice:	Wave good-bye, Billy! Don't you know it's rude to leave without saying good-bye?

CONVERSATION #7

Mom: How are you doing with the mail, Billy?

Me: There's an awful lot here. It's really piled up. But I don't see anything urgent.

Mom: What's in the shiny envelope?

Me: Something from Dad's office . . . It's an invitation to the Mardi Gras.

Mom: Oh, no.

Me: It has a handwritten note at the bottom, from June.

Mom: Is she kidding?

Me: She says you both have to go. It's going to be better than ever because she's the chairperson this year.

Mom: Who is she kidding? Doesn't she know we're sick here?

Me: It looks like she really wants you to go.

Mom: We'd have to put costumes together. . . . And see all those people . . .

Me: Breathe, Mom. Breathe.

Mom: You don't want to go, do you, Bill?

Dad: No.

Me: It says RSVP.

Mom: What is she thinking? She and her Mardi Ridiculous
        Gras.

Me: *Mmmmmph-pheeww.*

Mom: *Mmmmmph-pheeww.* It says RSVP? Will you take
        care of it?

Me: There's a card and envelope inside. I'll take care of it.

Me: Do you want to sit quietly together again, Dad?

Dad: (Silence.)

Me: (Silence.)

Dad: All right, I'll go.

Me: What? You want to go to June's party? You feel
        well enough to go?

Dad: I have to go.

Me: Wow . . . that's great news. I'll tell Mom. Maybe
        she'll go too.

Voice: Maybe she'll go too? I don't think so.

Me: You're not talking about the party, are you?

Voice: It's a big, big party, Billy.

Me: Are you going to be all right, then?

Voice: It's a big, big party, Billy. Like an open house.
        Everyone who's anyone shows up. Eventually.

CONVERSATION #8

Voice: Why don't you rest for a while, Billy?

Me: Me?

Voice: Yes, close your eyes and contemplate peace.

Me: Okay. What about Dad?

Voice: What about him?

Me: Is he closing his eyes and contemplating peace too?

Voice: He's going to get up in a minute and go to the kitchen.

Me: He's going to have something? Mom will be glad to hear that when she gets home. What's he in the mood for?

Voice: Hmmm. Something sweet?

Me: Yeah. Dad used to love sweets.

Voice: No. Something sour? Mmm, no.

Me: How about salty?

Voice: Salty? No. Something sharp? Yes, something sharp.

Me: Should I go help him?

Voice:	No, stay where you are and contemplate peace.
Me:	And he'll be all right then? He'll find what he needs?
Voice:	Peace.
Me:	Peace . . . But I—
Voice:	I told you to keep your eyes closed!
Me:	Wait! Dad, don't get up!
Dad:	Huh?
Me:	Linda . . . Linda!

THE INVENTORY

On the afternoon of February 25, I set Dad up to watch TV while Linda, Jodie, and I begin to gather all the dangerous objects in the house—medicines, sharp knives, sharp tools, razors and scissors, drain cleaners and other toxic chemicals, and rope or anything that could be used as rope—and hide them in a metal box that will go in the attic. We start in the utility room with the tools, then add my pocket knife and Grandpa Eddie's fishing knife, and then we move on to the bathroom cabinet. The pills Dr. Gupta prescribed in the fall were flushed long ago, but Jodie does the same with the white placebo sleeping pills. In the kitchen, we disagree about which utensils are dull enough to be kept downstairs for Mom to use in everyday cooking. Linda is standing by the utensil drawer with a carrot peeler and eight serrated table knives, I am testing the cheese slicer, and Jodie is holding the box and padlock. This is the way we look when Mom finds us and decides to go back to the doctor.

TACKING

We file into the office, Mom first, then Dad, then me. Linda and Jodie are home with Jodie's mother. Most of the lights are out in the waiting room, and the receptionist has gone home. We've been squeezed in at the last minute, the last appointment of the day. The sky outside the large windows is dark. A set of headlights illuminates the snowy hedge briefly before swerving out of the lot.

Fritz closes the door behind us. Our folder is right there at his fingertips and he had obviously been reviewing it before we came in. He bites his bottom lip and looks around at each of us.

"How's everyone doing today?"

I evade Fritz's gaze and open my mouth to speak. No sound comes out. Then the room starts to blur and swim, and a repetitive sound, between breathing and speaking, comes from the back of my throat: *Ah. Ah. Ah. Ah.* I force my knuckles into my mouth.

"It's okay, Billy. All sounds are appropriate here. Now take a deep breath. Deep breath, in and out—*mmmmmph-pheeww*—nice and deep, from the abdomen. What's been happening since I last saw you? Anyone?"

"I think I'm about to lose my job," Mom says.

"And why do you think that?"

"I'm not there enough."

"That must be very difficult."

"It is."

"It's been a while, hasn't it?" Fritz continues. Fritz clasps his arms over his woolly shirt and tries to get Dad's attention. He does a funny thing with his eyes, making them gentler, yet more powerful, like a kindly hook that tugs the truth out of you.

"How are you feeling, Bill?"

"He doesn't talk much anymore," I say helpfully, having dried my face with a Kleenex.

"Bill, are you having thoughts of harming yourself?"

Dad stares at his hands. I realize that he hasn't been shaving or trimming his beard. The different lengths of hair on his face make him appear rough, although he doesn't act that way.

Dad nods.

"How often?"

"Every day," Dad rough-whispers.

"Have you made a plan for killing yourself?"

"Yes."

"Bill!" Mom says. She reaches over and puts her hand on his arm.

"It's all right, Adele," Fritz says. "Everything is going to be taken care of. Your husband is going to get the proper care now." He writes something on a pad, then addresses us again. "I wish you had come in sooner," he says. Then he softens his tone a bit. "I'm really glad, very glad, to see you today." He says that in this hour he would like to speak with us individually, beginning with Dad.

Mom and I go out to the waiting room while Dad stays in with Fritz. We don't look at each other, but I sense Mom not wanting to let go of him, as if she could *shoosh* through the solid material of Fritz's door and be in there. She jumps up immediately when Fritz calls her name. Dad paces around the waiting room, and I find myself rubbing my hands too. Then I go last.

"Billy, tell me in your own words what's been going on at home."

He waits while I say nothing.

"For instance, describe what yesterday was like."

"Well, I came home from school. . . . And we watched a show about home remodeling on TV. . . . And I sat with Dad for a while. The voice inside Dad's head was telling him . . . to harm himself. To do away with himself."

"And you spoke to the voice?"

"Yes, to the voice."

"Not to your father?"

"No. They're two separate things, really. Two separate entities."

"Does this voice speak through your father? Can you hear it out loud?"

"No, I figured it out by listening to him. It's in his thoughts. It's trying to take him over and control his thoughts. I can guess what he's thinking."

"Like mind reading?"

"Yes." I'm pleased at how surprised he is.

"You're very close to your father, aren't you?"

"Right now I am."

"And you've worked very hard to take care of him during this time. Your mother has too."

I nodded.

"But I have to be very clear and firm with you, Billy:

You can't ever know for sure what someone else is thinking."

"You can't?"

"No. You can get information from what they tell you, you can look at body language, you can develop hunches that you might later be able to confirm. But you can't actually ever read someone's mind."

He keeps watching me, staring in that strange way, holding me in his gaze, and though what he's saying sounds like he's judging me, his eyes are saying he's seen everything before, everything. That noise starts again: *Ah. Ah.* And I think it's outside me, in the room itself, before I can feel that it's coming from me.

We just sit there for a few minutes, me struggling to control myself, then finding I don't have to, Fritz holding me with that gaze. After a while I stop looking all over the room and gaze back at him, like a staring contest but better. He says he will meet with my parents now to decide what's to be done.

"We're all here," he says when my parents come back. He smiles at Dad, writes very quickly, then smiles at Dad longer. "We need to start doing something for you, Bill, right away."

"Yes," Mom says, "we realize that. We'd like to resume treatment immediately."

"In terms of treatment options that remain, the time we've lost means we're now severely limited."

"I think that at this point . . ." Mom takes a deep breath. "Knowing what we know now, I would be much more amenable to putting Bill back on meds."

Dr. Fritz rests his elbows on Dad's file. Then he rubs the bridge of his nose. "What I mean to say, Adele, is that we don't have time to try another medication. We need something that acts more quickly. I have some calls in for you to look into electroconvulsive therapy."

"Wait a minute," Mom says. "Let's slow down here."

"What is it, Adele?"

"Please don't tell me you're considering shock treatments," Mom says. "Please don't tell me that."

"This may be a difficult decision, Adele. Do you want Billy to be present during this discussion?"

"He can stay here for now." This time Mom isn't saying she wants me here to take notes. I heard her telling Marty that she just doesn't want me to be alone.

"Well, let's not say 'shock,' Adele. It's an ugly word, and it shocks the patients. This sort of treatment isn't really what you're picturing. It's much gentler than it was years ago."

"Wait. Let's go back as if the last few weeks never happened, and start where we were before. We'll try another medication. Which one were you going to recommend next?" She feels on top of her head for her glasses, as if she's going to be given another prescription slip to read.

"Adele . . ."

Dr. Fritz seems a bit tired of Mom, as if he wouldn't mind never seeing her again. Has she become a medical obstacle? But he tries hard to hide it. "We're running out of time here, so we may need to continue this discussion over the phone. Adele, I'm always pleased when my patients and their families take an interest in their own care. I know you're all trying to be good consumers in trying to find what you think is best for Bill.

"But when we're dealing with a suicidal patient, time is extremely important. Your original psychiatrist, Dr. Gupta, doesn't generally supervise electroconvulsive therapy herself, so we will need you to meet with a different psychiatrist. I'll give you the name of someone with whom I occasionally cooperate. I've worked with him a few times over the years." He opens a drawer at the left side of his desk, pulls out a business card, and hands it to Mom. Doing so gives him a chance to stand up. He remains on his feet and so, even though nothing has been resolved, we realize it's time to stand up too. A massive tiredness hits me. I wouldn't care if I wasted my life sleeping.

Fritz walks us to the door. "Make an appointment with him right away—for no later than the day after tomorrow. I'll phone him to let him know you're coming. It isn't a hundred percent sure that this will help, but if it does work, it could start to help very quickly. And this time you *must* follow the treatment plan. I'll check in with you. And him. And you again."

Fritz chuckles. He sounds like the old Fritz. The Fritz who said, "Welcome!" to us and made us laugh by the door that day. That good day.

LITTLE GREEN HOUSE

Little green house, half an inch square. I've kept it in a tissue, in the toe of a sock, in my sock drawer. It's hollow. It fits on the end of my pinkie like a cap. Ten houses could dance on the fingers of my hands like finger puppets in a hurricane, but I've only kept one. If I set it on my palm the two long lines in my skin swoop in to make a driveway.

A molded plastic house made in a factory somewhere. It's made of one piece, with the details pressed outward. The chimney is just a button. The front and back of the house are identical, with a door smack in the middle and a window on either side. The two other sides have no features, no windows or doors, just a sharp line that shows you where the roof ends. How simple. How nice. Someone made a plastic house. I cup the house in my two hands, cover it, and blow on it. My breath is warm and it warms the house.

Oh, God of houses and lots. Oh, great monopolizer.

Protect this house. Whoever and wherever You are. Whatever You have the power to do. However You are able to know all our names and our streets' names. Whether You are watching from far away, like heaven, or from somewhere closer, like a low-flying helicopter. Don't turn Your back on us, okay?

People's luck is always changing. You made us that way. But You meant the bad times to be brief, didn't You? So why are our troubles hanging on?

Don't let our four walls collapse. Don't let our floor drop into the center of the earth. Don't let the air poison us. God of houses and lots, watch over this house.

MACARONI AGAIN

It's almost the end of lunch when I sit down with my tray. Gordy is out sick, and I plan to eat alone to avoid unwanted peer contact. I took my time leaving class and visiting my locker and stopped twice, without really needing to, in the bathroom so the food line would be almost closing when I got my plate of mac and cheese. I found a table on the outskirts of the room where I could sit by myself. Actually, there is one other person at my table—a stooping guy with a stubbly jaw, in a white uniform and a cloth cap that resembles a dinner napkin. He's the worker who sets up and removes the food in the steam tables, and he's taking a short break.

"How's the macaroni?" he asks. Despite the hat, his professional interest gives him a kind of dignity.

"Pretty creamy. You should find better tomatoes, though."

"You know how it is," he says. "They go with the cheapest stuff they can find. Every place is like that."

I heard a rumor that this guy, Ray, has an alcohol problem. I wonder if he deliberately went looking for a job in an institution in which most of the people have never had their first drink. Maybe it makes him feel safe. Innocent, even. Like he's one of us, just starting out in life.

I wouldn't go so far as to say that we're two peas in a pod, but our sitting together seems right. Ray and I, Ray and me. Not really innocent, but two guys who've been batted around by life. The drunk tank, the shock treatments, the carnival jobs and the cafeterias, maybe one or two eviction notices, desertion, disappointment, we know it all cold, and what I don't know I can imagine. Bits of a song enter my mind, a blues song, Ray's blues, and I wish I knew him well enough to try it out loud.

They don't like what I'm dishin'

No, not they. *She.*

She don't like what I'm dishin'
She (something something) bad
She only knows she's missin'
What she never should have had.

Well, this is real life, baby,
It's what's cookin' everyplace,
And if you don't like what I'm servin'
Find someone else to feed your face.

I'm not sure that captures Ray, though. I don't think he would turn mean like that at the end. If his wife or girlfriend were dissatisfied with him, he'd be more the type to just live with it, grateful for what he had.

The first bell rings and the shuffling starts—just a few sneakers at first, then hundreds and hundreds of them, an orchestra of feet. Mitchell and Andy walk by in the crowd. Andy spots me and stops, but I shake my head, look down at my plate, and wave him along. For once he does the right thing: He keeps moving.

WAITING

Mom, Dad, and I sit in the waiting room of a highly recommended psychiatrist. Everything in the room is perfect, telling us we are lucky to be here even though we don't want to be. Mom begins to chatter, pointing out that the walls are an intriguing gray or silver color, neither bright nor dull, but rich with layers. Each chair is like its own museum exhibit, with skyscraper lines and aggressively rough cloth, rough brown cloth for a poor monk to rest on, or maybe a rich person who thinks that too much comfort looks cheap.

A metal cube in the middle of the room, like a coffee table for astronauts, holds magazines in neat stacks just out of reach. Mom takes the half step needed to pick up a copy of *Architectural Digest*. I don't know what kind of impression she'll make. She hasn't washed her hair today. But we are only background. All our effort was put into the presentation of Dad.

Dad is shaved and trimmed. Dad has lost seven more pounds and is wearing a pair of my pants because none of his fit. Dad is pacing the space-age room with his hands in his pockets because the doctor is five minutes late for our appointment.

There's no reception desk to welcome us. One door in the waiting room is the one we just came through—it leads to the elevator lobby. The other door is made of dark wood with a stainless-steel handle—thoughtfully, the long, handicapped-accessible type—and it has no markings. No sounds come from behind the door, but we sense that behind this door is where the doctor is hidden. Having paced for seven minutes, Dad tries the door.

"No, not yet!" a voice calls sternly. We glimpse a bald head and a dark suit. Dad closes the door quickly, as if he'd walked in on someone in the toilet. He resumes pacing.

We three glance at each other. I crush my arms over my chest and slide way down on the rough seat, pretending to sleep. Mom tosses her magazine back to the table. It lands on the floor, so she gets up and places it neatly on the top of the stack. Not a sound comes from behind the door.

Another several minutes, and the door opens again. There's the doctor—bald, black suit, one and a half heads shorter than Dad and me. His office is painted a shade of gray that Mom would call pewter, with shiny black furniture. The wall behind his desk displays some precisely spaced three-inch photographs in yard-high black frames. We're inside now, so we quickly forget about the wait.

Dr. Mieux has an electronic notepad in the center of his desk. He holds the stylus over a screen as thin as a sheet of waxed paper.

"I'm seeing *all* of you?" he says, staring at me.

"Billy's helping me gather information," Mom says. "He has a very good memory for doctor visits."

I hold a pen over my own notebook. I too can document.

"I understand you've been feeling agitated, Bill," the doctor begins. He looks down at the tip of the stylus, then up again. "Bill? Aren't you going to answer my question?"

"I don't think you asked a—," Mom points out.

"Please! Mrs. Morrison! Allow the patient to speak for himself!"

"My father doesn't talk much," I say.

"He has to talk," Dr. Mieux says, watching the screen, "or we won't get anywhere."

Dad peers at Mom and begins rubbing his hands. "What do you need to know?"

"How long have you been feeling this way?"

Dad swallows hard. "About three to four months."

"And you've tried antidepressants? Which ones?"

Sliding and thudding noises have started in the waiting room, and there's a knock at the door.

"Yes?" the doctor calls. He lays down his stylus. He glances at his watch and smiles for the first time.

A man in a brown workman's coverall and cap leans his hand, shoulder, and arm into the doorway. "We've got everything up," he says, gesturing backward with a gloved thumb.

"Superb!" the doctor says. He gestures at the three of us. "You'll have to go back out to the waiting room for a bit. I'm taking delivery on a new set of furniture."

"Go back out?" Mom asks. "Now?"

"It won't take long," the doctor says.

We file back into the waiting room, where two immense packing crates now occupy most of the space. The magazine cube has been pushed into a small corner of the room, and the skyscraper chairs are squeezed around it at odd angles. We sit down in the available chairs, Dad facing the wall and Mom and I with our backs to him. Mom rests one foot on the cube, pushing a stack of magazines onto the floor.

"Oops," she says.

A second workman helps the first slide the largest box into Dr. Mieux's office.

"This isn't going to make it," the first man says.

"Why don't you take the door off the hinges?" suggests Dr. Mieux.

I exhale loudly, letting my head weave from side to side like a balloon running out of air. The second man kneels on the floor with a screwdriver. Dr. Mieux stands between us and the workmen, creating a visual barrier. He blinks at me to let me know I shouldn't be watching. Mom's foot starts bouncing on the table, while Dad continues to face the wall.

The workmen are highly efficient. The first packing crate goes into the office. Ripping, thudding, and sliding sounds follow. The men pass through the waiting room with the crate again, but this time they're walking backward. One of them presses the elevator button. The elevator dings. For a while the waiting room is quiet, except for the sound of drawers opening and closing in Mieux's office.

Soon the elevator dings again, and the two workmen enter, discussing a hockey game. One of them is carrying a bottle of soda. He takes a huge gulp that makes his Adam's apple seem like it's becoming dislodged. They squeeze through the office doorway with the second crate. This one appears much heavier. Then ripping, thudding, and sliding.

"Is this some kind of joke?" I ask Mom. "It's so unprofessional."

"Be patient, honey," she responds, waggling one foot.

I get up to check Dad. He's completely still, with his eyes closed.

"That's not right," the doctor says. "Let me look at the bill of sale. . . . No, I see, it's all right."

More sliding. Then the sound of padded blankets being heaped together. *Thwop, thwop, thwop.* The workmen walk past us with the second crate. Then they reappear carrying the office door. They attach it to its hinges. One workman tests the motion. Smooth. Mieux closes the door, and we don't hear any more sounds from his office. The workmen leave, the one carrying his soda bottle. Out in the hall, they wrestle the second crate into the elevator.

The situation is now exactly the way it was when we first came in, except that the waiting-room furniture is in disarray and crowded into one section of the room. Dad gets up and opens the door to Mieux's office.

"No! No!" Mieux cries. He has been arranging objects in the desk drawers. He rushes to the door and presses his body weight against it while Dad still has his hand on the handle. "I'll call you when I'm ready for you."

I cross over to Mom's seat and whisper, "Why don't we get out of here?"

"Shhh."

Dad paces around the room while rubbing his hands. He's trying to get interested in some of the art that hangs on the walls, stark black-and-white photos of shadowy mountaintops and of ice floes settling into abstract shapes. Dad walks up to them one by one. He used to do some photography and painting. He went to art school, on a full scholarship.

The door opens.

"I will see you now," the doctor says, nodding as if he's meeting us for the first time.

We take our places opposite Dr. Mieux at his desk. The stylus and screen are ready, but he doesn't use them. Instead, he folds his hands on the desk.

"First of all, we need to establish some ground rules if we're going to work together. You need to know that what just happened in *my* space was none of your business." He looks at each of us, but most sharply at me. "The boundaries between doctor and patient are absolutely paramount in this office. Is that clear to everyone?"

I respond by making my eyes go defunct, which he can interpret any way he likes: that I'm bored, that I hate him, or that I think he's a fake.

"Yes, of course," Mom mutters. Dad nods.

"Now let's get back to your situation, Bill." The doctor examines a few pages of records sent to him by Dr. Fritz. His black, perhaps ebony, desk and chairs have been replaced by another set. The surface of the wood has parallel waves too beautiful to have been painted by a human hand. If I didn't despise his furniture by association, I would trace one wave with my fingertip. Dad would have loved this.

The doctor sees me looking. "It's bubinga," he says. Then, to Dad, "You've tried a couple of antidepressants, with poor results. And there is suicidality?"

"What?" Dad asks.

"You sometimes think about killing yourself."

"Yes."

Dr. Mieux holds Dad's records between us. "Look, Bill, if you would like me to authorize this treatment you're requesting, I'm going to have to have you in my care round the clock—in order to monitor your progress and forestall any problems."

"I don't understand," says Dad.

"This type of treatment is generally available on an inpatient basis only. In cases where there is suicidality, it's best to have the support system in place, trained staff, monitoring . . ."

"You mean . . . a hospital?" Dad asks.

"Wait a minute," Mom says. "Why don't we discuss the options? We haven't even decided if we want shock treatments yet."

I plant my feet one at a time as loudly as possible, as if I am a giant with giant feet in giant boots.

Okay. Let's go, Mom. Let's just go. Thank you for your time and everything blah blah blah.

"Billy," Mom says, "would you rather wait outside?"

The doctor narrows his eyes at me and then continues. "Yes, a hospital. Hospitalization. You would be on my floor, getting the best possible care, under my direct attention. People come from all over the world—some very prominent people, members of royal families, although patient confidentiality constrains me from saying exactly who—from all over the world, to be on my floor."

But I'm not hearing this—*inpatient, hospitalization*. I'm hearing *the mental ward*. Restraints, barred windows, icy baths, screams at two a.m., disturbed people surrounded by other disturbed people who frighten one another with their delusions. How would Dad survive there?

And Mom looks like she's thinking, *If I put him in, will I ever get him out again?*

"I'm not sure that would work," Mom says. Her voice wobbles while she twists her necklace of wooden beads. "We haven't decided if we want shock treatments."

"This isn't cosmetic dentistry, Mrs. Morrison. This isn't something you choose or don't choose. You can't dillydally among the treatments, comparing caps and crowns and whether you should bond or whiten. Your husband is at risk of harming himself."

"We can take care of him at home."

The doctor refers back to Dad's record. He speaks to Mom without seeing her. "You've had him at home for—how long is it?"

"Almost four months," says Mom.

"And he hasn't gotten better in all that time. . . ."

"We're taking fine care of him at home." Mom's nervous, and her voice is up and down all over the place.

"You want him to get better, don't you? You don't want to be negligent." Mieux is staring at Mom now. "If the worst happens . . . It's ten past five, Mrs. Morrison. We have only a few minutes to make a decision here."

"I'm not putting him in the hospital," Mom says. "That's all there is to it. I'll see what our choices are. Maybe we'll leave the country and seek treatment elsewhere. Perhaps we'll try Canada, or Mexico. But he's not going into the hospital."

Why don't we just go then, Mom? Why don't we just up and leave?

I rise.

Ignoring me, Mieux writes a few comments with the stylus. He touches up the comments. He frowns.

"Well, I'm willing to try it this once, to supervise your husband as an outpatient. Keep in mind that I'll be paying very close attention to this case, to make sure it's handled correctly."

"I appreciate that, but let's not get ahead of ourselves," Mom says. "We haven't decided on anything. I need to know more. How do these treatments work, if they do work? We have no idea what to expect!"

Mieux sighs. He gets out of the chair and goes to a

cabinet with an empty vase on top. He gives Mom a brochure. *ECT: A Powerful Tool for Change,* by L. F. Mieux.

Mom hands the brochure to me and tells the doctor she'll call back after she's had a chance to review it. I clap my notebook shut with only a few lines filled. Mom and I leave with Dad between us.

In the parking lot, when Mom searches her purse for her car keys, her hand is shaking. I secure Dad gently in front, but once in the backseat, I slam my door loud enough to echo off pewter walls.

"Not now, Billy."

"You know what I'm going to say then, don't you?"

"Nothing, Billy. Not a word until we get home."

"I didn't like him," Dad says.

Back at the house, I escort Dad inside while Mom waits in the driveway. She'll be leaving again to get Linda.

"I'm not closing off my options, Billy," she says when I come back out. "We may want to continue with him. I checked with someone I know at the college. He has a very good reputation."

"You can't put Dad in the hands of a nut job!"

"Don't be such an alarmist. So he's a little eccentric. A

lot of brilliant people are. He probably puts all his effort into keeping up with research and hasn't developed good interpersonal skills. In the academic world, at least, that's fairly typical."

"This isn't the academic world—he's supposed to be a doctor! You hated him yourself. Why are you making excuses for him? What about being a good consumer, like you always told us to be? What about shopping around?"

"Sometimes—" The lady next door is just getting home from work. Mom waves. "Would you keep your voice down, please?"

"You didn't think he was any good. You thought he was full of it. You wanted to turn around and walk out, the same as I did."

"Maybe, but I restrained myself. He has a very good reputation. We have to put our personal preferences aside. It's just something that we have to overlook."

"He treated Dad like he wasn't even a person. Like he was a prisoner or something. Like he had no will. He treated us like we were less than human. People like that should never be given any kind of power."

"It's irrelevant."

"Irrelevant?"

"So he's rude to the patients. So what? Does that really make any difference? It's like saying he can't do a good job because he's bald."

"He *is* bald. And obtuse and—"

Mom reaches for the handle of the car door. "Listen, Billy. When I was in grad school, there was a professor in the biology department that no one could stand to be in the same room with. He smelled bad, he insulted the other professors, and he distributed fliers saying the women's studies department should be cut because it wasn't a real subject. But you know what? He contributed to the discovery of an oncogene. The first step toward a cure for cancer. How many people do you think he helped?"

"But did any of the people with cancer ever have to meet him? I don't think so. This guy is a *psychiatrist*, for Christ's sake. He's supposed to know how to act around people."

"We can find someone else to be nice to us. We can *pay* someone to be nice to us. But we can pay *him* to do what he does."

The curtains move and Dad looks out at us. I hold up my finger to say "one minute."

"You'd better go in," Mom says.

"Well, I'm glad I'm not the one paying the bills. He's not getting one cent of my money."

Mom drops her head and rests both gloves on the car hood, as if she's watching her reflection, except that the car is really dirty. "Maybe I shouldn't have brought you with us," Mom says. "I thought you might be up to taking notes."

Not bring me? If I hadn't been there, who knows what might have happened? Dad might not have come home. He could be watching the world through iron bars right now.

"Now everything is getting too complicated," Mom says as if I'm not there. "I'm the only one who can decide."

"How will you decide? Everything we've tried so far has been a disaster. The other day I was trying to remember what Dad was like before he got sick, and you know what? I can't even remember. I can't remember my own father and he's not even dead, he's living right here in the house and sleeping down the hall."

"Go in. I'll decide. I'll look into it, and I'll decide."

I hold up my notebook. "We got that brochure, right?"

"That's right. Where's the brochure?"

ECT: A POWERFUL TOOL FOR CHANGE

- The wife of a former governor and onetime presidential hopeful calls the results of her regular ECT program "wonderful."
- The chairman of psychiatry at a prestigious medical school says, "Most people today in patient surveys say it's no worse than going to a dentist."

For nearly seventy years, electroconvulsive therapy has been used to restore depressed patients to health. What can ECT do for you?

- *Restore* your zest for life
- *Revive* your appetite and help you maintain a healthy weight
- *Release* you from insomnia so you enjoy a good night's rest
- *Return* your performance level at school or job, honing your "competitive edge"

Are you a candidate for ECT? Ask your doctor, and begin to harness the healing power of electro-convulsive therapy now.

"Oh, for crying out loud," Mom says.

RESERVATION

Now it's Mom who paces the house, trying to decide whether to go ahead with the treatments. She has already told Mieux that she will go forward, and Dad has had all the necessary prep work done. But she has misgivings. She carries the appointment card for Dad's first treatment. She folds and unfolds it so many times that it turns silky.

"Listen to yourself," I tell her. "You obviously have doubts. Why do you have doubts? Because you know he's a quack. He shouldn't be practicing medicine. He wouldn't care if Dad died in his office, as long as it didn't leave a mark on the furniture. You should have told him no in the first place."

Linda agrees. "Too risky," she says. "The things we did before, they didn't work, but at least they were safe."

"It's just a piece of paper," Mom says. "We can cancel at any time. We can just fail to show up, the way we did with Fritz. The situation only *seems* to be out of our control, see? They need to act like they're in charge, but *we're* the ones who are in control. We're the ones they need to show up."

RESOLUTION

Someone approaches the bike rack behind the library as I'm going in the entrance. He hovers near Triumph.

"My bike," I boom in my strongest voice, retracing my steps.

A middle-aged guy stands up. He's a little younger than my father, and he's wearing a peacoat with a plaid muffler.

"Beautiful bike. English, isn't it?"

"Yep." With the hand holding my keys, I point to a plate on the top tube that says MADE IN ENGLAND.

"I always wanted one of these. How does it ride?"

"Three years with no problems. And a lot of decades before that."

"They're a little heavy on the hills, aren't they? Have you considered putting a larger cog in the back?"

"I don't mind working up a sweat on the hills once in a while. I'm trying to keep it as intact as possible. I could use a springier seat, too, with all the potholes, but I just like the looks of this one." I wait for him to step away, but he doesn't go.

"It's in beautiful condition," he says, running his hand over the handlebars. "Have you ever thought of selling?"

"No, I haven't." That sounds ruder than I intended. "Sir, this is my primary mode of transportation."

"Well, I wouldn't want you to lose your transportation. I would give you enough to get another decent bike. How about three hundred dollars?"

"It's not worth that much."

"Then why don't you take the money?"

"It's not worth that to anyone else, I mean."

"How about four hundred, then?"

"Are you crazy? You can find five of them for that much on the Internet."

"Why is this bike so special to you?"

"It's practically my first bike. It feels like that, anyway. I fixed it up myself. . . . My father and I did." A light snow is falling, and I want to be inside.

"Well, it's really just what I'm looking for. And I have been looking on the Internet. Will you take my card, in case you change your mind?"

I wave the card away and go upstairs. Once inside the door I check back to see if the guy has his grubby hands on my frame again, but he's walking to his car. Four hundred dollars! Out of nowhere. It almost seemed like one of those situations they warn you against, when someone pretends to share your enthusiasms or offers to do you a big favor, and they're really a sexual predator attempting to get somewhere with you. The card and everything. Or perhaps he was the devil incarnate. He did seem to genuinely like the bike, though.

I go inside and find a computer carrel in the corner of the third floor, where I'm least likely to encounter other students from my school. I pass two guys a year older than me—"It's all right," one guy says, "it's just Bob."—who seem to be participating in a chat room. "Say you're a 40DD," one of them whispers to the other.

Four hundred dollars. I don't know whether I should tell Mom and Dad. On the one hand, it's a lot of money that perhaps we could use (I actually know very little about our financial situation), but on the other hand, I have no intention of selling. We do, after all, need my bike. With Dad out of commission, it's our second car. It allows me to do important errands like this. With the saddlebags, I could conceivably do grocery runs as well. Maybe I should offer to do something for the Brooksbie once in a while. Yes, I am sure they would not want me to sell the bike.

Tuning out the guys in the nearby carrel, I do a key-word search on the words "electroconvulsive therapy." The search brings up several websites with pleasant and soothing names like Personal Wellness, Web MD, Family Doctor, and the National Institutes for Health. I print up a page of questions and answers from Family Doctor.

What conditions does electroconvulsive therapy treat?
Electroconvulsive therapy (also called ECT) may help people who have the following conditions:

- Severe depression with insomnia (trouble sleep-ing), weight change, feelings of hopelessness or guilt, and thoughts of suicide (hurting or killing yourself) or homicide (hurting or killing someone else).

- Severe depression that does not respond to antidepressants (medicines used to treat depression) or counseling.

- Severe depression in patients who can't take antidepressants.

- Severe mania that does not respond to medicines. Symptoms of severe mania may include talking too much, insomnia, weight loss or impulsive behavior.

How does ECT work?

It is believed that ECT works by using an electrical shock to cause a seizure (a short period of irregular brain activity). This seizure releases many chemicals in the brain. These chemicals, called neurotransmitters, deliver messages from one brain cell to another. The release of these chemicals makes the brain cells work better. A person's mood will improve when his or her brain cells and chemical messengers work better.

What steps are taken to prepare a person for ECT treatment?

First, a doctor will do a physical exam to make sure you're physically able to handle the treatment. If you are, you will meet with an anesthesiologist, a doctor who specializes in giving anesthesia. Anesthesia is when medicine is used to put you in a sleeplike state. The anesthesiologist will examine your heart and lungs to see if it is safe for you to have anesthesia. You may need to have some blood tests and an electrocardiogram (a test showing the rhythm of your heart) before your first ECT treatment.

How are the ECT treatments given?

ECT may be given during a hospital stay, or a person can go to a hospital just for the treatment and then go home. ECT is given up to 3 times a week. Usually no more than 12 treatments are needed. Treatment is given by a psychiatrist.

Before each treatment, an intravenous (IV) line will be started so medicine can be put directly into your blood. You will be given an anesthetic (medicine to put you into a sleeplike state) and a medicine to relax your muscles. Your heart rate, blood pressure, and breathing will be watched closely. After you are asleep, an electrical shock will be applied to your head. The shock will last only 1 or 2 seconds and will make your brain have a seizure. This seizure is controlled by medicines so that your body doesn't move when you have the seizure.

You will wake up within 5 to 10 minutes after the treatment and will be taken to a recovery room to be watched. When you are fully awake, you can eat and drink, get dressed, and return to your hospital room or go home.

What are some side effects of ECT?

Side effects may result from the anesthesia, the ECT treatment, or both. Common side effects include temporary short-term memory loss, nausea, muscle aches, and headache. Some people may have longer-lasting problems with memory after ECT. Sometimes a person's blood pressure or heart rhythm changes. If these changes occur, they are carefully watched during the ECT treatments and are immediately treated.

What happens after all of the ECT treatments are done?

After you have finished all of your ECT treatments, you will probably be started on an antidepressant medicine. It is important for you to keep taking this medicine the way your doctor tells you to so that you won't become depressed again.

I ride home standing on the pedals instead of sitting on the seat. I take the route that allows me to coast down long hills. Triumph, it's going to be all right!

At home, Mom is checking the maintenance bills for Brooksbie while Dad allows Linda to give him a cucumber facial. I drop the printouts on Mom's lap and she reads them quickly, her lips moving at certain key words. I was surprised that the treatments didn't sound that bad. It looks like Mom might be right to go ahead, although I would never tell her so. When she's done, she chucks me on the head and holds up the appointment slip like it's a winning lottery ticket.

VACILLATION

But the night before Dad's first treatment, I bike back to the library on the pretext of returning some books. The computer carrel I used last time is available. After all these months, is our problem really going to be solved so easily? I get on the Internet and search for the phrase "shock treatments."

The results that come up are different this time. In addition to pleasant-sounding organizations like Healthy Place, there are many more with worrisome names such as Antipsychiatry.org and Ban Shock, as well as groups such as the Committee for Truth in Psychiatry and the Foundation for Truth in Reality. I click on an article called "ECT and Brain Damage: Psychiatry's Legacy," posted by a group called Say No to Psychiatry!

The story of electric shock began in 1938, when Italian psychiatrist Ugo Cerletti visited a Rome slaughterhouse to see what could be learned from the method that was employed to butcher hogs. In Cerletti's own words, "As soon as the hogs were clamped by the [electric] tongs, they fell unconscious, stiffened, then after a few seconds they were shaken by convulsions. . . . During this period of unconsciousness (epileptic coma), the butcher stabbed and bled the animals without difficulty. . . .

"At this point I felt we could venture to experiment on man, and I instructed my assistants to be on the alert for the selection of a suitable subject."

Cerletti's first victim was provided by the local police—a man described by Cerletti as "lucid and well-oriented." After surviving the first blast without losing consciousness, the victim overheard Cerletti discussing a second application with a higher voltage. He begged Cerletti, *"Non una seconda! Mortifiere!"* ("Not another one! It will kill me!")

Ignoring the objections of his assistants, Cerletti increased the voltage and duration and fired again. With the "successful" electrically induced convulsion of his victim, Ugo Cerletti brought about the application of hog-slaughtering skills to humans, creating one of the most brutal techniques of psychiatry. . . .

Electric shock is also called electroconvulsive "therapy" or treatment (ECT), electroshock therapy or electric shock treatment (EST), electrostimulation, and electrolytic therapy (ELT). All are euphemistic terms for the same process: sending a searing blast of electricity through the brain in order to alter behavior. . . .

ECT is one of the worst and most permanently destructive methods used by psychiatry. Before heavy tranquilizers and muscle relaxers were used to render the patient completely immobile, shock treatments often caused broken vertebrae due to the severity of the force involved with electric shock. There is nothing mild about this "treatment." Slick advertising campaigns and glossy brochures cannot turn this very harmful procedure into a useful and safe one.

If a psychiatrist or mental health "professional" tells you that ECT is safe, ask him or her to let you watch as they themselves receive a "treatment." Their negative response should set your mind straight on the subject. If they do consent, then I suggest getting away from them as quickly as possible—they truly must be crazy as a loon to accept your proposal!

The website quotes Ernest Hemingway and claims that the reason he shot himself was that shock treatments destroyed his mind. "Well, what is the sense of ruining my head and erasing my memory, which is my capital, and putting me out of business? It was a brilliant cure but we lost the patient."

Antipsychiatry.org has a page called "Psychiatry's Electroconvulsive Shock Treatment: A Crime Against Humanity." At the top of the page is a photograph of a woman in a hospital gown, strapped down to a table, with some kind of bit in her mouth. Wires on either side of her head lead to a box with switches and dials, where two hands wait, seemingly about to throw the switch. Because the woman's mouth is forced open by the bit, you can't tell if she's trying to shout for help. She might be.

Some psychiatrists falsely claim that ECT consists of a very small amount of electricity being passed through the brain. In fact, the 70 to 400 volts and 200 to 1600 milliamperes used in ECT is quite powerful. The power applied in ECT is typically as great as that found in the wall sockets in your home. It could kill the "patient" if the current were not limited to the head. The electricity in ECT is so powerful it can burn the skin on the head where the electrodes are placed. Because of this, psychiatrists use electrode jelly, also called conductive gel, to prevent skin burns from the electricity. The electricity going through the brain causes seizures so powerful the so-called patients receiving this so-called therapy have broken their own bones during the seizures. To prevent this, a muscle-paralyzing drug is administered immediately before the so-called treatment. Of course, the worst part of ECT is brain damage, not broken bones. . . .

Defenders of ECT say that because of the addition of anesthesia to make the procedure painless, the horribleness of ECT is entirely a thing of the past. This argument misses the point. It is the mental disorientation, the memory loss, the lost mental ability, the realization after awaking from the "therapy" that the essence of one's very *self* is being destroyed by the "treatment" that induces the terror—not only or even primarily physical suffering. ECT, or electroshock, strikes to the core personality and is terrifying for this reason. . . .

Since the "patient's" fear of ECT is one of the

things that makes ECT "work," psychiatrists often get results by merely *threatening* people with ECT.

I print out my findings. I take them into the men's room so I can read them in their entirety. I could throw them away, right in this wastebasket under the paper towels, before I leave the library. I could keep quiet about what I know and just watch Dad for signs, hover above Dad's situation like a guardian angel. What would be the point of showing Mom, anyway? We have no other options on the table. We have Plan A but no Plan B.

When I get home, Dad has gone to bed to prepare for an early start in the morning. Mom is drinking tea and staring out the window over the sink. I doubt she can see anything out there, with lights on inside the house. I hand her the printouts. They're crumpled, damp, and probably unsanitary. Mom puts down her mug and begins to read them, with one hand at her throat. For a long time she doesn't react.

"Not Hemingway!" she eventually gasps. I knew that would get to her—Mom's master's was in American studies.

She shakes her head and leans against the counter. She touches the necklace my father gave her when they were poor. We could be poor again.

"You may not show any of this to your father or your sister."

"You have to cancel the appointment, Mom."

She rinses the mug and puts it in the dishwasher without saying anything.

"Right? Mom? You have to cancel the appointment, or they'll turn Dad into a zombie."

"I'm not going to cancel it."

"But look what happened to Hemingway—and all those other, ordinary people. Their minds got wiped out. Anything that was special about them—pfft. And even anything that wasn't special."

"Billy—"

"Come on, Mom! *Where's that phone number?*"

"Shush." She lays her hand on my arm, but I knock it away.

"Don't shush me! I won't be shushed anymore!"

"If you yell and act agitated, you'll just make things worse. Don't you want your father to get some rest before his first appointment?"

"So you're going, then? You're doing this to Dad? You don't even want my opinion."

"I want your opinion, only in a lower register."

"I won't let you do it."

"Oh, really? How will you stop me?" Mom steps backward. A bag of recycled Brooksbie papers blocks her path, and I don't even warn her. She doesn't fall, though.

Mom has no idea that in the last five minutes of my bike ride I developed a secret plan. If she decides to go ahead with this, I'll take Dad away. The nights are getting warmer—we could live in a tent on Plum Island. Any court in the United States would see it my way.

"Billy," Mom asks me after a while, "what percentage of your father would you say is still there?"

"Maybe thirty," I answer. "But at least it's something."

"That's exactly the figure I was going to give."

DAWN

My social studies teacher, Mr. Misuraca, distributes a test up the aisle. He moves like a trained bear, and every test, no matter what the alleged subject, ends up being about the nineteen sixties.

Brenda Mason strokes the shoulder of her sweater as she writes her name on the test, almost as if she's patting herself on the back.

I write my name but nothing after that.

They leave the house at dawn.

They stop for coffee at Dunkin' Donuts, but Dad isn't allowed to have anything. Mom puts two honey-dipped Munchkins in a wax bag for later, should Dad choose to accept them.

Uncle Marty drives because Mom and Dad were up most of the night, and Mom's too tired to drive. In the passenger seat, Mom navigates with the map.

The landmarks of Route 1 pass their windows. A

lighthouse, a ship, and the tower of Pisa, all of which are really restaurants. An orange Tyrannosaurus rex that guards a miniature golf course. They've seen it a hundred times, but this time it startles them, and they wonder whatever possessed someone to put it there. Questioning, questioning.

The traffic doubles and redoubles. The Boston skyline ascends, gathering memories of family trips around it like a broad gray skirt.

Coolidge Hospital is the size of a town. Marty follows signs for Building G. He drops Mom and Dad in front, then goes to park the car.

They sign in at the front desk.

They take the elevator down to the basement.

The basement is a plain, concrete-walled clinic.

Dad is wearing his snappy first-day-of-school clothes.

The other patients are all in pajamas and bathrobes, because they're living here.

A nurse calls "Bill Morrison," and Dad looks up.

He and Mom are shown into a second room.

In the second room is a new doctor they've never met before.

He and a nurse take Dad into a third room.

Dad lies down on one of three beds.

The nurse straps him in and gives him an injection.

His body relaxes and his eyes close.

The nurse smears something on Dad's head.

She places an oxygen mask over Dad's mouth and nose.

The doctor presses onto Dad's head two circles attached to a wire.

He seems to be asleep now.

The doctor throws a switch.

May God forgive me.

That I would do nothing while a doctor sent fire through my father's body.

TREATMENT REPORT: DAY 104

A current passed through Dad's brain, producing a seizure that lasted thirty seconds. His arms and legs never moved, but his fists clenched involuntarily and his toes twitched.

Inside Dad's brain, neurons resembling tall, thin trees stood in groves. Their spidery branches were intertwined, almost touching. Lightning shot from tree to tree and from branch to branch, making the bare wood rattle and hiss. This lightning had the power to revive or destroy whatever buds of thought or nests of memory ever lived there. Dad's soul walked at the base of the trees, fearful and wondering. Some branches were cut and fell to the ground like dry kindling. Others crackled, swayed, and absorbed the shock, eventually becoming still.

THIS —

Is this my inheritance? Red hair, blue eyes, and a dark place in the mind that will call me when my time comes, and I will have to go there?

Like a church bell, a factory bell, or a funeral bell?

I am (after all) Bill Junior.

part three

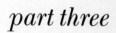

TREATMENT REPORT: DAY 109

Dad has completed three sessions of electroconvulsive therapy, each of which has obliterated his memory of the past twenty-four hours and taken with it some of his other mental abilities, too. In other words, he is even more less-smart than he was from not sleeping, although we hope that one day he will become more smart again.

THE DARK SPACES

"Sixteen across: patella."

Dad and I are doing the newspaper crossword on a Saturday afternoon while Mom reads a magazine in her chair in the corner. When he was well, we would time ourselves on the crossword puzzle—usually thirty minutes, once as low as twenty-six minutes, thirteen seconds—but now we're taking all the time we need, not looking at the clock.

I give him a head start before I make my suggestion. "Okay, how about 'kneecap'?"

Dad begins writing in the squares. N-E-E.

"Wait! There's a *k* in 'kneecap.'"

"Where?"

"At the beginning."

He erases what he's done and starts again. The word fits.

"Does 'needle' also have a *k*?" he asks, trying to find the pattern.

"No, it doesn't. But 'knead' does, like when you knead dough to make bread. And remember, 'know' does, as in 'I know you.'"

He nods. "I'm pretty sure I have that one."

None of the articles mentioned that the treatments would cause Dad to lose—temporarily, we hope—his ability to spell. But I see it each time we do the crossword puzzle. The first time I noticed it, I felt embarrassed for Dad. Maybe I even pitied him. But now my reaction has changed. For the most part, I feel curious and just basically interested. Because the articles I've read say nothing about this problem, I feel like I've discovered something. I strangely enjoy watching him and looking for trends in what he does and doesn't remember. Still, it seems a little cold. I excuse myself by deciding it's the kind of thing he himself would find interesting, if it weren't happening to him.

A car goes by the picture window, up our hill. Mom lays down her magazine and waves. "The man who stopped in yesterday just went by," Mom says.

To help Dad with his memory loss, I've developed a technique I call "backgrounding," and Mom helps me implement it. With this technique, we assume that he remembers nothing, and we fill in for him as much as we can. Normally, Mom might have said just, "There he is again!" about the passing driver. But with my background-ing program, she beefs up her comment with a short reference to yesterday's meeting.

"Someone stopped in yesterday?" Dad asks.

"Yes," she answers. "We were just getting out of the car, and he pulled in the driveway. He was thinking of buying the house at the top of the street, and he wanted to know how long we had lived here and what we thought of the highway noise. You were very honest with him and said it bothered you, but we explained that you were a light sleeper and I'm a heavy sleeper."

"Uh-huh," Dad says, waiting to see if the information resurfaces in memory. Sometimes it does, and sometimes it doesn't. But in giving Dad that information, Mom is treating him as if he can step back into the conversation once he has the background. He can still participate. I call that technique "normalizing."

"He must be serious about buying if he's back again today," Dad says. "Did he say whether he was a light sleeper?"

"No, he didn't," Mom says. "He mostly listened to us."

"He's probably not light then," Dad continues. "Or he would have mentioned it. Maybe he's in-between."

If only Hemingway had had someone to background his short-term memory. Would things have turned out differently for the American novel?

AN AMBIGUOUS STATEMENT

Dad stands at the living room window with his back to me. It's 5:20 p.m. on March 16.

"The days are getting longer," he says.

I'm rereading an old *Newsweek* in the easy chair. "Dad, is that longer-good, as in more natural light/more time to enjoy activities, or longer-bad, as in you can't wait for the day to end?"

Dad looks at me, then turns back to the window.

"The days are getting longer," he repeats.

The house is quieter now after school. Linda and Jodie have disappeared from the afternoons and are now meeting at Jodie's house. They left behind clumps of brown paper wadded with ink, and some burnt ceramic scat that may have been beads that stuck to the oven when I wasn't paying attention. I didn't have to clean up because Mom said I should take it easy for a while.

But beyond that, there is a sense of peace in the house,

though I can't put my finger on it exactly. Dad's right—the days *are* getting longer. Could that have been what went wrong with Dad, that the days were getting too short? Might the light box really have worked, if we hadn't been so quick to discontinue it?

But thinking this way doesn't do any good. We had another follow-up visit with Dr. Fritz, and he said that although, again, he wished we had come back in sooner, we shouldn't be kicking ourselves, because to a certain extent we were just doing the best we could with the tools and resources we had at the time. But it seemed to take a lot of effort for him to say this, and while he said it he looked at our file and not at us, not staring at us at all, as if he didn't like us anymore, and this made us feel worse.

For Saturday lunch the day after his sixth treatment, Dad ate a ham sandwich, a hard-boiled egg, a quarter of a melon, and a piece of chocolate cake. Mom and I eyed one another and kept bringing out more food.

SOLILOQUY

Reading in bed that night, I find this section in Walter Merig's *The Progression of Major Depressive Disorders*.

It is perhaps ironic, therefore, that the greatest rates of morbidity occur when the patient appears to be getting better. This seemingly paradoxical phenomenon can be traced to two developments: first, that the patient may have wished to self-terminate much earlier and did not have the physical strength, powers of resolution, and planning resources to do so, resources which are now, with some improvement, more easily at his command; and second, that the recovering patient, now viewing the illness from "the other side of the hurdle" as it were (Femmigant, 1998), regards the recently concluded illness with his improved perceptive powers as a torturous ordeal, the recurrence of which must be avoided at all costs.

I sit up and reread this a few more times, allowing its meaning to unwind in my tired brain. We were happy to see Dad getting better. We high-fived each other over him finishing a ham sandwich. But now he's in more danger than he's been in the past four months? Still . . .

I get out of bed and pace across my room. What do we do now? Do we try to keep him at this level? Do we try to prevent him from getting any better? Do we hope that he stays just sick enough that he never sees the big picture? That he concentrates on surviving day to day and never looks back to realize how terrible it was?

It's a philosophical problem, isn't it? If the risk of suicide is greater as you recover, would it be better to stay at least a little sick—let's say an easily controlled low-grade melancholy—and live longer but not as well? Or would it be worth it to end it all on the up cycle, savoring the taste of hot French toast with maple syrup? The brightness of a tube of aquamarine? The feel of salt spray? I imagine Dad as a ski jumper. He sees the mountain slide away beneath his feet, then fade into the distance. He decides never to come back down.

When did I pick up Dad's habit of pacing? I have to calm down and get back in bed. I have to stop being theoretical.

I have to remember that I'm not a philosopher or a psychologist, I'm a son. This is Dad I'm talking about, not some experiment, not some patient in a book. Of course he has to keep getting better.

And even though I'll say, "Whoa! What's your hurry?" when in the next few days he talks about getting out his paints or stopping by the office to say hello, I can't get in the way of his recovery.

ANATHEMA

Except that Dad hates the treatments.

Hates the way the other patients look, wan and stick-like in their bathrobes. Hates the wheelchair he rides from the treatment room to the car. And especially, hates the moment when he lies down, waiting to be knocked out so his mind can be taken out of his control and . . . not wiped clean, but smudged around the edges, the way your sweater sleeve smudges words off a chalkboard.

INTROSPECTION

Every once in a while I come across Mom standing in the kitchen and twisting her necklace. She might be steeping a teabag or sorting through the mail. She doesn't show much on the surface, but I can tell by the way her eyes aren't seeing what she's looking at that she's pitching a silent, internal horror fit over the fact that we almost lost Dad. I wonder exactly what she tells herself at those times. I could break into her thoughts at one of those moments, engage her in conversation, but to be perfectly honest, I would rather not know.

SWEETS

The cute girl in our bakery hands me the price list. Mom has given me "carte blanche" to buy whatever we need for the celebration of Dad's eighth and last treatment—whatever looks good, she says. A fancy cake two or three times as much as we can eat, maybe some cookies or Italian pastries on the side. Linda has already bought the party decorations and hidden them in her room. Uncle Marty and Jodie have been invited.

Cannoli are always good, and chocolate-chip cannoli are even better, although both get soggy if you don't eat them the same day. I crouch in front of the case to get a better look at the cakes waiting for other customers, and I see, along with my own reflection, a boy's birthday cake with sky blue frosting and *Star Wars* figures—Darth Vader and Luke Skywalker facing off with their lightsabers. Too theatrical to be appetizing. I like the golf-themed cake better. It's covered with green-tinted shredded coconut that resembles grass and dotted with mini-marshmallows for golf balls. Beside it is a dignified white-frosted cake that says "Best of Luck Stan" in a circle around a small plastic adding machine, possibly for someone who is an accountant.

Needless to say, there's no precedent for our specific occasion. I look at the price list again. Color photos of sample decoration styles, with a variety of messages, are ranged along the top. Are we a "Good Luck"? A "Congratulations"? A "You Did It"? "Happy Last Treatment" would be too specific, and "It's Over" is too vague.

While I'm making up my mind, the loud and distorted electronic doorbell over the bakery door rings: *bwing-bwong!* A woman enters the store and speaks to the girl and her father, the baker. It's June. Not the month of June, but June from Dad's office. The scent of her perfume mingles with the bread-and-sugar air in the bakery. I curl into a cannonball position in front of the case, hoping she won't recognize me.

"Billy!" She stoops toward me and I straighten up.

"Hello, Mrs. Melman."

"How's your dad doing?"

"A little better, actually."

"Fantastic. Will he be coming back to work soon? We

have a temp working at his desk. A nice kid, but he seems to have accidentally deleted half the files on Bill's computer. Maybe he thinks that will make us keep him on longer. But tell Bill that as soon as he gives the word, we'll clear things out and give the temp his marching orders."

"Well, I don't know how soon it will be. You better wait to hear from him. See . . ."

"Yes?"

"See, we've sort of had a routine."

June searches my face. "You had a routine. Routines can be good."

"Yes."

People on the outside don't realize how tricky a situation like this can be. You don't want to rush things. You don't want to upset the delicate balance that causes a sick person to get better. It's not like you just decide that someone will improve and they do. Mom was right when she called her "easy-breezy June."

June pays for the Stan cake and gives the girl a two-dollar tip, even though there's no tip cup. She turns back to wave to me on the way out the door and catches the baker studying her rear view. She smiles and waves to him, too.

I pick out both a golden raspberry-filled cake with

buttercream frosting for twelve and a Boston cream pie. The bakery can stack the two cakes in a corrugated crate for me to carry home. I watch the girl's father move my raspberry cake to a work counter. Then he adorns it to my specs: "Congrats Dad" plus balloons and ribbons drawn in every frosting color they have, exuberating around his name and cascading into heaps on the cardboard plate.

SHRINKING

The night before Dad's eighth treatment, I walk him around at midnight while Mom takes a rest. Dad *really hates* the treatments.

"I can't get back on that table," he says.

"You have to. It's all planned. They're expecting us."

"Why don't you call them, early in the morning, and let them know we're not coming."

"We can't, Dad. You have to go. Just one more. Then never again. Then you can relax. I promise."

I'm as tall as Dad, and my arm feels good where it rests along his bony shoulders. My outside hand holds his wrist so I can suppress any rubbing compulsion. We look like a couple about to begin a square-dance maneuver.

I feel alert and happy tonight. Although it seems strange, I'm realizing that these have been good times. I've felt occupied and useful, and I've never spent so many hours with my father. But now our togetherness may have peaked—he's been talking about going back to work again.

No one can deny that Bill Junior has been there when needed, like Mom's uncle Jack, who fell into the tight squeeze in Normandy in World War II by standing under a blanket filled with air.

Will life be cutting me down to size now? I feel my regular life, boring, disappointing, and mediocre, tugging me back with a hundred strings. It wants to turn me into a two-inch-high toy parachute man who will sit in a drawer until someone takes him out again. Folded, rubber-banded, put aside, waiting.

SYNONYMS

Saturday morning we sit outside Dr. Stone's office at Coolidge Hospital, waiting for Dad's last treatment. Mom and Uncle Marty know the place well, but Linda and I have never been here before. Our family, including Dad, are the only people in street clothes. The rest are bathrobed inpatients. Dad keeps to himself, while Mom and Marty exchange a few words with the patients around them. The cast of characters changes a bit every time, Mom explains. Two patients that she used to talk to regularly, Mike and Irene, have finished before Dad and gone from the hospital. She wishes she could find out how they're doing.

This time, when the assistant calls Dad's name, Dad makes a brief announcement to the other patients. "I won't be seeing you again after today. So, good luck to you all." He waves over his shoulder to them and to us as the double door to the treatment room swings closed behind him.

Twenty minutes later we are waiting for him to wake up when Dr. Stone calls Mom and Uncle Marty into his personal office.

"Should we stay out here and wait for Dad?" Linda asks.

"Let's all go meet Dr. Stone," Mom says. "It's a special occasion."

Dr. Stone is a thin man in a polo shirt with a bandage on the side of his forehead. This gives me the creeps, as if he's been operating on himself. The office is clean and bare, with just a dinged metal desk, a few chairs, and filing cabinets. There's no decoration except for two Harvard Medical School diplomas and a photo of him running the Boston Marathon, stringy and determined in a pair of very small shorts.

"It's gone very well," he says. "You should be pleased." We are.

"And you're seeing improvements at home?" We think so.

"He's put five pounds back on," Mom says. "And he got out his camera and started playing around with it."

"Very good," Stone says. He opens the schedule book he shares with his assistant. "I think another two to four treatments are all that will be needed to really lock it in."

Mom and Linda both fold their arms tightly over their

chests and recross their legs. Each has a leg swinging. Marty blinks as if he didn't hear right.

"I may be mistaken," Mom begins, "but I seem to recall hearing from you that this course of treatment would require eight visits total." She strokes the earpiece of her reading glasses slowly through her hair.

"Eight was a very good estimate," Stone says. "We've often had very good results with eight. The remaining two or three are just a bit of insurance, to make sure the improvements really jell."

"You're telling me," Marty says, "that my brother's brain has to jell?"

"Well, not his brain really, but the changes in his brain. If we want them to become permanent. We want them to coalesce, to firm up, to be cohesive. To really take hold, to lock in."

He keeps going, looking for a word we will accept. I would hear more about his reasons, but I am gone.

CORRIDORS

Water sears my eyes. I run blindly through corridors, left and right, right again, taking enough turns that I hope never to find my way back. The hallway is a moving watercolor of white, pink, and chrome.

"Paging Dr. Billy!"

I turn around to find Linda cupping her hands over her mouth and pinching her nose. She drops her hands. "Big brother," she says in her normal voice.

"*Incompetent. Just—incompetent.* I promised him he wouldn't have to come back here again."

"Well. Was that even your promise to make?"

We walk together until we come to an open door.

"Those idiots have no idea what they're doing. How many times did I try to tell Mom that this was a bad idea?"

Linda leans against the doorway. "Be quiet, Billy. God is here."

Inside the hospital chapel, the organist is playing the hymn that goes to the tune "Finlandia." We know this song from Dad's music collection—"Be still, my soul: The Lord is on thy side"—but the organist keeps stopping at a bad time to practice this phrase or that. We sit down and Linda bows her head, but I keep my head up and look around, at the dark paneling, and at the one narrow stained-glass window that a crowded city will allow.

While I may have called to God in moments of desperation, I still don't believe in Him. See, I have this deal with God: I don't believe in Him, and He doesn't believe in me. In fact, we view each other the way you might view fictional characters. We hear good things about each other, but we would never expect to see proof of each other's existence, either in a random meeting on the street or as a name on a tombstone.

Mom believes that there's a happy afterlife for everyone, even those who may not seem to deserve it, like murderers, terrorists, and pedophiles. Linda believes that anything you do will be forgiven, if you ask the people around you or ask God. Now that we bought the cake and the decorations and the gifts, I wonder who will be the one to tell Dad that his treatments aren't finished.

We return slowly through the zigzag of corridors. The halls are clear and distinct now, alive with workday sounds. We get to the waiting room, where Mom sits with Marty and the other patients. Marty goes to the swinging door that separates this room from the treatment room. He stands there until Dad comes in smiling, about to raise his arms in triumph.

"You sit, Adele," Uncle Marty says. "I'll tell him."

"Tell me what?" Dad asks.

Marty turns Dad's wheelchair toward the hall.

"Let's go for a walk, bro," he says.

DECELEBRATION

Linda keeps the decorations in her room that night. But we cut up the raspberry cake. And in spite of the lack of reasons to celebrate, the cake tastes good. *Really* good.

A READER'S QUESTION

Q: Does Dr. Mieux, the psychiatrist with a taste for fine furniture, ever reappear in this story?

A: No, he does not.

MARTY

Marty says he had a rough time telling Dad, as he puts it, "about the more treatments." When he talks to me in the driveway after the cake, Marty looks like he's falling through the ice again, into the cold place where no one but Dad wants him. "He was disappointed, but he kept telling me not to feel bad," Marty says. "He was worried more about *me*."

Throughout Dad's sickness Marty has seemed convinced that Dad was always thinking about him. His money problems, his business schemes, his trauma over the divorce from Aunt Stephanie . . . I got the idea that Marty was kidding himself, feeling all this sympathy from Dad that couldn't possibly have been there. That he was filling Dad with intelligence and other good qualities, like a little kid confiding in his teddy bear.

But along with the quiet and calmness that seeps into the house, something else seems to be happening for real.

It's like Dad was a snow globe that had no top on it, and all the stuff that was inside had somehow disappeared. Now it's as if the top has been put on and something is falling to the bottom, settling and collecting, flake by flake. Some recognizable stuff that can only be called the Spirit of Dad.

AN EXISTENTIAL MOMENT

Pudge starts calling the house nearly every day, outside of Mom's work hours. One day he hints that the museum is about to go under, and that her job will be at risk unless she takes responsibility for raising a big heap of money from the members. Mom talks to him from the kitchen for half an hour, pleading and arguing, but never in the taking-charge voice she uses on most people.

"If it's phone work, I'll do it," she says. "If it's e-mail, I'll do it. Tell me what I can do right now, Pudge. Tell me what I can do from home, without going in. I can get a laptop. Working from home, I can spend unlimited hours on the phone, and I will get you that money."

"It's extortion," she says when she hangs up. "He's actually threatening to fire me."

"Why don't you go in, Adele?" Dad says. "Go in in the mornings once in a while. I can take care of myself."

"What would you do by yourself in the morning?" Mom asks him.

"Read the newspaper, watch TV, listen to the news . . ."

"The news is so depressing, though," Mom says.

"I could always call Marty if I need someone to talk to."

"That's an idea. In fact, why don't we see if Marty is willing to come over a few mornings a week while I go in to work?"

And so our daily pattern begins to shift. Mom will go into the office from ten to noon a few days a week, as well as working three hours a day in the afternoon. Because Marty's bar/restaurant mostly needs him in the evenings, he can come by mornings most of the time. Dad will also stay home alone for an hour here or there, with the understanding that he will call Mom or Marty if he becomes agitated or needs company.

The first morning that Dad is to spend some time by himself, I see him rubbing his hands a little. Not in the old automatic, repetitive way, but more of a light buffing for good luck. It seems that he could use a booster, a dose of the old empowering phrases we used when he was really sick. But as of this moment we've dropped all the old techniques and are relying entirely on shock treatments to make Dad better. So, technically, I shouldn't do this anymore. Since Mom is just a few feet away gathering the museum's financial records, I decide to come at it indirectly.

"You know, Dad," I begin, "everything is for the good."

"Everything is for the good? What in the world do you mean?"

"That everything is for the best. Ultimately. In the universe. It all works out, you know. Like a kind of perfection. Even your having been sick, I guess. Maybe some good will eventually come of it. It all happens for a reason, as part of some massively perfect scheme."

"You know, you can't believe everything you hear, son. The fact that someone said something and it sounded catchy doesn't mean it's true."

"What are you two talking about?" Mom says, putting a ledger book in her briefcase.

With one finger, Dad pushes Mom's glasses farther up her nose. "Whether the universe is moving toward perfection. Which in your case it clearly is."

"Well!" Mom says. "That's so sweet." Mom actually blushes, and I sort of want to leave the room. From what I can tell, this is the first time in a long time that Dad has said something in a husband-type way rather than as someone who needs her help, and I wish I hadn't been here. He used to say poetic things to Linda, too. Like "Anon there drops a tear . . . for the cold strange eyes of a little Mermaiden and the gleam of her golden hair" (Matthew Arnold).

"I would say no, Billy," Mom says. "The universe doesn't seem to be moving toward perfection. At least, I don't see evidence that that's happening. It's just something people say when they're desperate. Something they grab at when they're drowning. I'm not sure those little sayings really work."

"But Fritz thinks they do, right? And we're back to Fritz again. I mean, he's back up on the pedestal. He's God now because Dad is getting better."

"Fritz isn't God. Can't you get through a single conversation without wallowing in sarcasm? He's just a regular person, but he seems to know what he's doing. Don't think of him as God. Think of him as a tool we can use, which is what that idiot Mieux is, and what they all are."

I leave for school thinking of a line from "Desiderata": "No doubt the universe is unfolding as it should." At first it seemed like more of the same, but it really isn't. It doesn't say the world is headed for perfection or destruction, just that it is going in the direction it's intended to go. Old Max Ehrmann was obviously hedging his bets there.

TREATMENT REPORT: DAY 128

Marty has been having such a good time talking to Dad (or *at* Dad would be more accurate) that he has decided to take complete responsibility for Dad's remaining two or three treatments. Although Marty usually closes the bar and cleans up at two a.m., he is changing his schedule and retraining himself to get up at five. This allows Mom to add more mornings to her workweek.

COMING UP NEXT

"Dad! Come on!" I shout.

I turn on the TV in the den and settle into my side of the couch with a bowl of cheese curls. I move the ottoman with my feet so it's in just the right spot. Dinky accordion music plays, and the camera pans across a wall of canvases. The paintings show windows, crystal glasses, and chandeliers, all painted with starry highlights.

"Dad! It's starting!"

Dad stands in the doorway with the newspaper while the Light-Teacher begins his introduction: "Even if you've never held a paintbrush. Even if you've never learned to draw. You can become a—"

"Billy! What are you watching this for?"

Dad blocks my view as he switches off the TV. Then he goes back to the living room to read.

ADOLESCENCE: IDYLLIC OR INSIPID?

Mom tells me to plan on another follow-up session with Dr. Fritz. After school on Wednesday afternoon, I am expecting Mom to pick up Linda, Dad, and me. Instead, Marty pulls up at the house, and after killing the drive time with a story about a bartender who may be stealing, he drops me off at Fritz's by myself. Although I've been to Fritz several times now with the family, in the waiting room the old nervousness comes back. Why am I being seen by myself, when Dad is the one who's sick? Why am I being placed under the microscope? Or is Fritz going to ask my advice in planning the rest of Dad's treatment? Mom mentioned some talk of trying another antidepressant once the shock treatments had started to take effect.

Here is Fritz in his lumberjack clothes. Here is the photo of Fritz's sailboat. I sit down opposite his desk.

"How are things going with you, Billy?" Staring. He likes me again!

"All right, I guess. Dad seems better."

"And how are you, apart from how your dad is doing?"

"Fine. Tired, maybe."

Fritz links his hands over his chest. "I asked you here, Billy, because your parents, in particular your mother, are concerned with how you are recovering from your father's illness. Do you have any idea what she might be talking about?"

"Not really."

"Well, from what she's told me—and correct me if I'm wrong—you seem to be having trouble letting go. You still spend a great deal of time at home. You don't seem to be, as I might put it, *reengaging* with life. Could there be any truth to that?"

I decide to withhold my own stare from Fritz. Instead, I look at the photo. Two guys out on the open seas. Well, that's one kind of adventure. But with all I've been through, how could anyone say I haven't been engaged with life?

"Look, Fritz, I mean Dr. Fritz. I just want to make sure everything goes okay—I mean, that things don't get worse again. My mother is all into her career again, and there has to be someone looking after things at home."

"And does that person have to be you?"

"Well, who else is there?"

"Who else is there? You tell me."

"Tell me, Dr. Fritz, how is your sailboat? Is she a good seaworthy vessel? Does she win you any big sailing races?"

Dr. Fritz tilts his head and smiles slightly. "That isn't my sailboat, unfortunately. Billy . . . You have to let go of caring so much for your father and get back to normal. That would be better for him, and for you. Do you have any reason not to let go?"

"I already told you that someone needs to stay home."

Fritz presses both sets of fingertips onto the closed file detailing the problems of my family. It's as if he's saying it's simple, it's self-explanatory, it's all there . . . but you're not allowed to read it.

"It's praiseworthy that you have such feelings of loyalty, Billy. I can understand your anxiety about all the difficulties you've been through recently. But I don't think you have to be so afraid anymore, now that your father is getting adequate care. Can you accept that?"

There is this folder, my life, with a big hole in it that everyone is talking about.

"Billy? Can you accept that?"

I'm studying the sailboat photo again. All at once I realize, after all these visits, that the colors and the clothes in the photo date it by about forty years. The person I thought was Dr. Fritz is a lookalike, probably Fritz's father, and the small boy is Fritz himself. For some reason, this makes me tremendously sad.

"So I really do wonder what is prompting you to occupy so much of your time with your father and his illness."

I nod. I know something bad is happening to my face.

"I guess . . . I just don't think I'll ever do anything this important again."

"You think helping your father is important. Is anything else in your life important?"

Every thought seems to have left my head, as if I just woke up or was just born.

"Deep breath, Billy. *Mmmmmph-pheeww.* Now tell me. What else do you think is important?"

"I used to think writing songs was important, but now I don't know anymore."

"You don't know anymore."

"No."

"What are some of the things you've been missing out on since your father became ill?"

"Having music in the house, really loud, bouncing off of everything."

"Having music in the house."

"*Having music in the house.*"

"What?"

"Dr. Fritz, you're repeating me."

Fritz just waits, doesn't rise to the bait.

"And maybe seeing my old friend Mitchell."

"This friend Mitchell, what is he like?"

"Oh, sort of fat. A big brain but doesn't care about anything. Sarcastic. Makes fun of everything, laughs at everything. Thinks everything's funny."

"Does he make you laugh too?"

"No. Not right now, anyway. I'm not in the mood for him now."

"Well, tell me, Billy. Is it any more true to say that everything is serious than to say that everything is funny?"

"Could you repeat that, please?"

"Is life so serious?"

"Well, that's easy to say now. It's easy to laugh and joke afterward, when everyone is safe. You yourself seemed to think everything was serious just a few weeks ago."

Fritz raises one hand, a variation on his old "Welcome" gesture. "Look, why don't you call this friend and make some plans?"

"Because he isn't serious enough. I could never tell him what happened to Dad. He would never understand how serious that was."

It's warm in the office, but I pull the zipper of my parka way up to my chin.

"If you do spend time with Mitchell or other friends, does it have to be serious?"

I picture something sparkling on the ground—a piece of treasure that turns out to be a gum wrapper. Those are my heroic moments, turned to ribald jokes for Andy's amusement. My Best Of's turned to America's Funniest.

"I guess I could just see him but not tell him what happened."

Fritz nods, a rolling nod, three times. "You can do that, or you can do something else, whatever you feel most comfortable with."

"I guess—the thing about Mitchell—I don't think he's really suffered in his life."

"Do you know that for sure?"

"No, but I think if he did I would have known about it."

"Maybe."

We sit for a while not saying anything.

"Why don't you reconnect with him and see how you

feel? Try reconnecting with all the things you used to like about your friend Mitchell."

"I don't like thinking about it that way."

"Then just call Mitchell."

BOULEVARD

In East Hawthorne, near where Gordy lives, is a wall about waist-high that stands between a broad sidewalk and the harbor. I'm showing it to him because everyone from the old regime knows it's the perfect wall to walk on. He pulls himself up easily and begins cantering along the top.

"Have you ever thought of riding your bike up here?" he asks.

"I've thought of it, but never actually done it. I don't think anyone has."

"Maybe you can be the first."

An elderly woman in a black nylon tracksuit stops a few yards away and glares at us.

"Sorry, ma'am," Gordy says, hopping to the ground. Then to me he says, "I guess it isn't very polite to walk on a wall that's inscribed with the names of dead fishermen."

"Everyone does it," I tell him. "She should be glad

someone's taking an interest. Let's jump back up as soon as she's gone."

"That's all right," Gordy says. "I've experienced it."

"Say, Gord."

"Say, Billy."

"I was wondering: Did she say anything particular? At the very end?"

"At what end?"

"You know, when she died."

"My mother?" Gordy looks out toward the water.

Now I wish I hadn't brought it up. Maybe I should have kept my mouth shut. Maybe the answer is something really horrible like "I can't breathe."

"Not really. She was in and out. She said a few things like that I should work hard and have goals and try to do something with my life. The typical things parents say."

"Except that this time you felt you had to pay attention?"

Gordy laughs and steps up onto a metal railing while still looking out to sea. The white sun of early April is reflected in one curve of the harbor, making it look like a bowlful of snow. "Yeah."

"Is that why you're good at stuff, because you work hard?"

"I don't know."

Tactical error. I shouldn't ever let on that I admire him. If I say something like that again I bet he won't want to be my friend anymore.

"I'm just trying to make some plans, you know? I'm just trying to decide what to do next," I explain.

But I already know—I can almost tell by the texture of the way my brain feels most days—that I am not cut out to do a lot of things well. One thing, maybe. One big thumper of a thing. The type of thing that will earn me a gravestone with just three words: I DID THIS.

STIRRING

Two a.m. Everyone's asleep. Everyone but me, that is. Linda's passed out under her mad photos and her Garfields. Someone in Mom and Dad's bedroom is snoring like a pack of wolves. But I'm wide awake.

Why can't I have the sleep that I deserve? Did I get so used to being up at night that I forgot how to sleep? Is something nagging at me? Have I forgotten to do something? Then it comes back.

Why does a man feel tired
Why does a man feel dead
When misfortune comes to misery
Comes to (something) in his head

It's a world of trouble, baby
Oh Mister Trouble, let me go
Get your fingers off my (something)
And leave me to my—radio?

STRIVE TO BE HAPPY

"Hello?"

"Mitchell?"

"Yes?"

"It's Billy."

"I know this."

"Promise me one thing, okay?"

"What's that?"

"That you won't ask me any questions."

"I will not ask you any questions."

"Okay, then. Do you want to come by after school tomorrow?"

MISSING

For the first time in a long time, I've overslept. Sleep filled me up so completely that I actually felt myself getting taller. The clock reads 8:37 (it's Thursday, though—good, not a treatment day), and Linda's standing in the doorway to my bedroom.

"Billy," she says, "Dad's gone."

"He's gone? Where is he?"

"I don't know. He's just gone."

She leads me down the hall to our parents' room and opens the door. Mom is asleep with her mouth open and her arm flung over her eyes to block the bits of daylight that creep around the curtains. Dad's side of the bed is empty. Linda pushes the door open a bit more, making it creak, and Mom sits up and says, "Where is he?"

"Oh, Mom," Linda says. "He's gone."

"What do you mean?"

"He isn't anywhere in the house."

Mom gets out of bed and puts on her bathrobe. We move softly into the main rooms. No one, not even Linda, is getting hysterical, and that makes it scarier somehow. The calmness is something fearsome. That's how accustomed we are to Dad's actions/communications/requests/needs being part of our consciousness. With the house so quiet and nothing to advocate for or resist, we're like astronauts working around the capsule whose lifeline somehow becomes unattached. We're floating out toward the infinite.

"Bill!" Mom calls into the hallway. No answer from the living room or other rooms.

Mom's face is grim. We follow her, like baby ducks, to the big bathroom, where she looks up at the shower rod. Nothing. Next she goes into the kitchen and stares at the floor around the oven. Nothing.

"All right," Mom says. "I'm sure it's all right."

Nonsensically, I open the oven door. Linda, even more nonsensically, peers into the microwave. Of course, nothing. Mom opens the kitchen curtains and looks into the backyard. Nothing.

Mom stops at the kitchen phone. She chews the inside of her mouth while dialing Marty's number. "Bill's missing. Is he with you? Can you call back right away?"

"We should fan out," Linda says. But we don't. I open the door to the den. The couch is there, empty, with the remote and some newspapers. It's as quiet as when we went to sleep last night, and I get a sick feeling that this room is historical, they all are—they can be preserved just the way he left them, a Museum of Dad.

"All right," Mom says again.

We go to the utility room and push aside brooms, skis, and tennis rackets. Mom pulls on a ceiling cord that brings down the ladder for the attic crawlspace. She scrambles up the stairs. The metal strongbox is still in its spot at the edge of the crawlspace. I hear Mom pull it onto her lap, shake it, and test the padlock.

"It's all right. It's all here," she says—the knives, the poisons, and the sashes of our bathrobes. Mom's bare legs reappear on the ladder, and her bare feet touch down quickly on each step.

"All right," I say.

"It's going to be all right, you know, Mom," Linda says. Her voice is getting trembly. "Either way, it will be all right."

"Either way?" Mom asks her.

"We'll still have each other."

"Honey . . ."

"Wait," Linda says. "What's this?"

Passing through the kitchen a second time, we see something we missed before, a folded sheet of paper resting on the counter by the bins of flour and sugar. It has one word on the front: "Adele."

"It's a note," I tell Mom. I pick up the paper, wanting to open it, but it's really Mom's, and so I surrender it to her.

"I don't know if I want to open it," she says. "Maybe you should leave me alone for a few minutes. No, on the other hand, stay here."

"Do you want me to read it first?"

"No, I'll read it." She unfolds the paper. I can see through the back that it contains only one sentence.

"Okay," Mom says. She turns the paper around so we can both see it. "Gone for a walk," it says.

We rush to our rooms and pull on yesterday's clothes. Put on our boots by the living-room door—it's mud season. Run to the driveway, where both cars are empty, and look up and down our hill to find more nothing. The highway is noisy since it's rush hour. We follow Mom into the backyard. Here is the plastic bench where Mom and Dad sit in summer, between the rosebushes, drinking store-brand diet cola and listening to the highway noise. Here is the statue of Athena, goddess of wisdom, lying on her side wrapped in a blue tarpaulin like a shroud.

We stop at the stockade fence that blocks our house from the highway.

"I'll run back there," I say.

I swing around the fence post and stagger into Mom's compost heap. A small ravine separates our yard from the highway itself. I cross it in a few wobbly steps. Then Linda is behind me, standing in the partly frozen compost. I scan the northbound and southbound lanes as cars whoosh by just feet from my rubber boots.

"I don't see him!" I call back to Mom.

Linda and I look at one another. A few yards away is the entrance to the tunnel. We stumble into the ravine toward the cement ring of the entrance.

"Where are you?" Mom calls from the other side of the fence.

"Just a minute!" Linda calls back.

We peer into the tunnel. It's four feet high, with eighteen inches of muddy water.

"He wouldn't do that," Linda says.

"Sometimes people do," I tell her. "They take pills or something and crawl in someplace small to die."

"Dad wouldn't do that to us. He wouldn't make us look for him here. He wouldn't do that to Mom."

"What are you two doing?" Mom yells. "Get back where I can see you."

I decide to concur with Linda. "We can come back. Later. If we have to."

The three of us run to the front of the house. Along our street neighbors are pulling out of their driveways to go to work, to take their toddlers to nursery school.

"We need a plan," I tell the other two. "Mom, you go uphill. I'll go downhill. Linda, you stay here and wait for the phone to ring." But I'm so agitated that when Mom starts to rush uphill I forget and go with her. Linda follows us too.

The woman next door, the shadow maker, is getting into her enormous van.

"Have you seen my husband?" Mom calls.

"I just got out here," the neighbor responds, chirpy and regular. "Have a good one!" At the front of her house a wind chime strums: *throm, blikblik.*

We clop down to the end of our street, lurching and lunging in our big galoshes. The only place to go is around a bend in the road. When we turn the bend, we see a wooded lot, the only spot in the neighborhood that hasn't been built on yet.

"What's that?" Linda calls out, pointing.

"It's him!"

Dad's between the trees, awfully still, with his back to us and his head at an angle.

"Bill!" Mom calls. She breaks into a sprint. "Bill!"

Are his feet on the ground? I ask the no one in my mind. *Tell me his feet are on the ground.*

Dad's eyes are closed, and he stands with his head cocked, hands in his coat pockets. His white tennis sneakers are inch-deep in spring mud.

"Bill?" Mom puts her hand on Dad's shoulder.

"Hello!" he says to all three of us, opening his eyes.

"Oh, Bill," Mom says. "We were so scared."

"Dad." Linda winds her arms around Dad and squashes her head against him. Just what I wanted to do. Mom leans on both of them, trying to collect some air.

"Bill, why didn't you tell us you wanted to go for a walk?"

"You were asleep," Dad says, "so I just went. I felt like going, and I went."

"You could have woken us up, Dad," I tell him. "That would have been no problem. I would have gone with you."

"You wanted to go by yourself?" Mom asks, standing on a dry patch and scraping one boot against the other.

"I'm all right by myself," he says.

"But you should have asked us to come," I continue automatically. "You might . . ." But I don't know what he might. Forget how to walk in traffic, and step in front of a car? Turn his ankle on a wet piece of pavement? Obstruct the progress of a school bus? Bump into someone's trash can?

"Why are you hiding in these woods?" Mom asks, looking around at the nearly leafless trees and the coals and cans left over from someone's beer party.

"Something called me in here," Dad explains. "Up there." He points to a spot in the crown of the trees, where a single branch jitters against a freshly washed sky. "Shhh. Listen!"

At first there are only the usual morning sounds of highway noise and slamming car doors. And then we hear it.

Trlrlrlrlrlrlrlrlrlrlrl.

Then a funny thing happens to Mom's face. She begins to smile, and the smile grows, exceeding what you would consider normal limits and turning into a half circle. It grows until it seems like it's taking up two-thirds of her face. Her cheeks turn into Ping-Pong balls, while her eyes get smaller and smaller. Then her eyes completely disappear.

I DECIDE TO BECOME A PSYCHOLOGIST

I never thought I would say this. But I have. Fritz showed me the way.

I've made many mistakes in my life so far. This experience with Dad is no exception. When I think of some of the things I've done, I pour a bucket of shame over my own head. Then I writhe in the shame.

But I learned that I have too much of something, and maybe I can take whatever it is that I have too much of, and instead of putting it all on Dad, I could spread it out usefully among many people.

Whatever that thing is, could I productively harness it? Could I distribute it to a different customer each time in a series of scheduled appointments? Could I channel it with a steady, Fritz-like gaze?

This might be a good time, then, to do some homework. Not the kind I usually do, but the regular kind.

Schoolwork. Whatever it is that's been weighing down my satchel.

THE ISLAND

Mom, you returned the library books and threw away the nutritional supplements. A muscle pulsed in your jaw, like a Morse code of regret. You were wishing for a do-over.

But we were like a family on an island, Mom. When we were on the island, we couldn't tell how big the island was, what its shape was, or how long we would be there. We couldn't know the island until we were in a boat speeding away from it. We can see everything, now that it's too late. *It was just a little island.*

Dad, you whistle a tune that sounds like music. You sound the way you did before, when you thought the world could be trusted.

Will we see the island again? If we do, will we all still be together, or will it be Linda or me alone? And who will spot it first? Who will be the one to say, "I've been here before. I remember that rocky beach and that shadow"?

But it's spring, and the sand is gone from the streets of our suburb.

Now fly, Triumph.